Seasons

of the

Four States

Missouri
Oklahoma
Kansas
Arkansas

Presented by

JOPLIN WRITERS' GUILD

Contributors

Marjorie Wood ~ Margarite R. Stever ~ Bonnie Tesh
Larry Wood ~ Howard Forsythe ~ S.V. Farnsworth
April Brock ~ Glynn Bennion ~ Catherine Valentine
Lindsey Hobson ~ Annie Lisenby
Billie Holladay Skelley

Publishing Coordinator – Sharon Kizziah-Holmes

Paperback-Press
an imprint of A & S Publishing
A & S Holmes, Inc.

ISBN -13: 978-1-951772-00-0

INTRODUCTION

When Joplin Writers' Guild president Summer Farnsworth (writing as S. V. Farnsworth) proposed in late 2018 that our group stage several writing contests throughout the year in 2019 and publish an anthology at the end of the year consisting of the best contest entries, I was skeptical because it was something the Joplin Writers' Guild had never done before. I and a few other members thought it might be a too-ambitious project for a relatively small group such as ours. Despite our hesitation, we voted to do it and to center the anthology around a seasonal theme. Well, here it is a year later, and we've pulled it off. Thanks largely to Summer, who served not only as the driving force behind the anthology but also as its editor, you now hold in your hands *Seasons of the Four States*, a collection of stories and poems by some of the best writers in the Four States region.

The Joplin Writers' Guild counts among its membership many excellent writers. Our group has always fared well in writing contests sponsored by regional and state organizations like the Ozark Creative Writers, the Ozarks Writers League, and the Missouri Writers Guild. The quality of the stories in *Seasons of the Four States* will give you an idea of why. However, our summer short story contest, embracing three different categories, was open to anyone living within a 75-mile radius of

Joplin. So, the stories contained herein represent not just the work of our members but also the work of other fine writers in the region.

The Joplin Writers' Guild is an affiliate of the statewide Missouri Writers' Guild, which was established in 1915 as an outreach of the University of Missouri's School of Journalism. The Joplin Writers Guild traces its origins to the old Tri-State Writers' Guild, which was active at least as early as the 1920s. In the mid-1940s, the Tri-State Writers' Guild affiliated with the Missouri state organization under a new name, the Joplin Writers' Guild, and the group has been in continuous operation under that name ever since.

The Joplin Writers' Guild meets the second Thursday of each month at 6:00 p.m. at the Joplin Public Library, and anyone interested in writing is welcome to attend. Our members vary from veteran writers with many published works to beginning writers just starting out. Dues are $10 a year, but visitors may attend up to three times before deciding whether they want to join.

The purpose of the Joplin Writers' Guild is to foster our members' development as writers and to recognize their writing achievements. Our meetings feature guest speakers, critiquing each other's work, and writing exercises and contests. For more information, visit our Facebook page at Joplin Writers' Guild - Facebook

Larry Wood, Vice-President
Joplin Writers' Guild

CONTENTS

ABOUT THE EDITOR
AND CONTRIBUTOR

S.V. Farnsworth is a linguist librarian who has spent time in Asia. Issues with grit give her multicultural novels the traction to move you.

Her debut novel, *Woman of the Stone*, book one in the Modutan Empire Series, is available for purchase in paperback and e-book worldwide. It is available for librarians to order, so be sure to request it.

She is writing book two in the Modutan Empire Series, *Monarch in the Flames*. It's an epic fantasy with an appeal to readers who connect with #MeToo concerns and admire strong female characters.

She graduated with a B.S. from SUU in 2002. She currently works at Crowder College as an ESL instructor. You will frequently find her at workshops on writing and book signings in southwest Missouri.

She has been elected as the 2020 secretary of the board for the Ozarks Writers League. She served two consecutive years as president of the board for the Joplin Writers' Guild, coordinated the 2018 and 2019 conferences, and edited the guild's 2019 anthology.

Subscribe to her newsletter for exclusive content and updates on her books at **svfarnsworthauthor.com**.

SEASONS

ADVENTURING WIND

MARJORIE WOOD

Sweeping from the North during winter.
Whipping across the cold tundra.
Whizzing across the northern plains.
Giving tingling, biting kisses in the Four States.

Climbing over the high mountains.
Rolling across the central plains during spring.
Whirling, spinning, violent vertical whirlwind.
In the wake, paths of destruction in the Four State towns.

Gathering moisture from the Gulf.
Snaking across the baked South during summer.
Slowing, leaving smothering heat and humidity.
Going silent and still in the Four States.

Crawling across the northern mountains.
Stealing from the trees during fall.
Howling though the bare branches.
Dancing with the colorful leaves in the streets of the Four States.

WINTER

WHISPER'S CHOICE

MARGARITE R. STEVER

Sleet beat against the windows like thousands of angry bees trying to break inside to the warmth. Whisper arose from her rocking chair and meandered to the kitchen. She filled her tea kettle with water and started to set it on the stove. A fierce pounding on her front door startled her, and the kettle clattered to the floor.

She flicked on the porch light and peeked out the window. The face she saw on the other side of the glass was the same that had haunted her dreams for ten years. She silently cursed her pulse that raced at the sight of the hulking blond man who leaned against her porch post. The memory of him down on one knee in front of a waterfall raced through her mind before she was able to stop it.

She cracked the door open. "Devon, what are you doing here?"

The muscular giant's blue eyes iced over. "We need to talk. Let me in."

Whisper heaved a sigh and swung open the door so he could enter. "What could we possibly have to talk about after not seeing each other for a decade?"

"It's Mom. She's had an accident."

All the breath whooshed out of her body at once. She felt woozy with fear for the sweet woman she'd known. "Come into the kitchen. I'll make some tea. Watch your step. I dropped the kettle when you knocked."

He chuckled. "You're still jumpy, I see. I used to think that was so cute." He grabbed the dish towel off the oven handle and mopped up the water on the floor while she refilled the kettle.

Whisper shook her head. "You used to think a lot of things were cute. Then you traded me for a different model."

"That's not what happened." He rubbed his temples.

She forced a measure of calm into her voice. "All I know is one day I was planning our wedding and the next you told me you never wanted to see me again. A wish I have respected."

He sank into a kitchen chair. "I guess I owe you an explanation, even if it's ten years too late. Sherry convinced me you were cheating on me with Jack Messer and stealing from Mom."

Whisper sputtered, "Jack Messer? I hardly knew him. And I would never steal from your mom. I'd never do anything to hurt her."

"I see that now, but Sherry was very persuasive. Mom's diamond bracelet came up missing, and she pointed the finger at you. She mentioned how you'd told Mom that it was lovely shortly before it disappeared."

"And of course, you believed her. You didn't even ask me about it, you jerk. Did the fact that she was your sister's best friend and had access to everything in the house even occur to you?"

"No. She'd been hanging around our house for so long that she was just one of us kids. She was always pointing out that your family was poor. She made me believe you only wanted me for my money and what you could get from my family." He ran his hands through his short hair. "I was already married to her by the time I figured out the truth. I found Mom's bracelet in Sherry's jewelry box several years later. It still had the 'Forever Yours' inscription from Dad on it."

She shook her head and wiped a tear. "It doesn't matter now. It's all ancient history. Tell me about your mom and why you drove all the way to Asbury, Missouri, during an ice storm to talk to me."

Devon studied his hands before meeting her gaze. "I wasn't going to come. I didn't want to see you."

"Oh, you sweet talker. Just what every woman wants to hear from her ex-fiancé." She crossed her arms over her chest and glared at him. "Get to the point."

"Mom was in a car accident and has a brain injury." His voice hitched.

Her anger drained away. "I'm sorry to hear that. What can I do? You wouldn't be here if you didn't need me."

"It's messing with her memory. All she does is

talk about her fabulous daughter-in-law. She's talking about you. She tells everyone who'll listen how wonderful you are. She can't understand why you haven't been to the hospital to see her."

"She thinks we got married? She really is confused. The poor woman." Whisper shook her head. "If she thinks I'm her daughter-in-law, who does she think Sherry is?"

"Sherry and I divorced three years ago. Mom never liked her. I think she blocked her out."

The tea kettle whistled. Whisper poured boiling water in two large mugs. "What kind of tea do you want? Lemon and ginger or peppermint?"

"Lemon and ginger is fine. Thanks." He accepted the mug and bounced the tea bag in the hot water.

She studied her own tea. "So, what do you want me to me do? Set her straight?"

"No." He leaned toward her with that intense look in his eyes she never could resist. "I want you to pose as my wife and go visit her."

She jerked her head up and narrowed her eyes. "You want me to what?"

"Pretend to be my wife. It'll make her happy to see us together, and what could it hurt?" His fierce gaze pierced her heart.

"Not what, but who could it hurt is the question. This is the first time we've seen each other since we separated. There is no us. There is you, and there is me. No us. How can you think lying to your mom about such a thing is a good idea? No. I won't do it." She gulped her tea to kill the sudden lump in her throat.

"Come on! After everything my mom did for

you, you're refusing to do the one thing that could make her happy? She wrote the letter of recommendation that got you accepted into art school. She cosigned on your first car. I can't count how many times she helped you work through girl stuff since your own mom was always too busy. She was always there for you, and you won't do this little thing for her? How selfish can you be?"

"Your mom means the world to me. I'll go visit her. I'll give her my love and keep her company, but I will not lie to her."

Devon finished his tea in two huge gulps. "Okay. I guess that'll have to do. Thanks. She's at Mercy Hospital in Joplin. We can go see her tomorrow if you're free."

"I'll consider going tomorrow if the roads aren't icy. I'm not going anywhere on bad roads. What if I call her tomorrow and go see her later in the week?"

"Yeah, that could work. I realize you don't have to do anything. Thanks." The big man rose to his feet and set his mug in the sink.

They heard a huge crash close to the house. Sleet and wind pummeled them as they hurried outside to see what had happened. They stopped short at the sight of the damage. An enormous oak tree had fallen on both of their vehicles. It had caved in the cab of Devon's truck and the back half of Whisper's compact car. Neither vehicle was going anywhere for a while.

Devon's mouth hung agape. "What are we going to do now?"

Shoulders slumped; Whisper trudged back into the house. She held the door for him and leaned against the living room wall.

"We need to call the insurance company, but no one can do anything until it stops sleeting. It's going to take a while to cut the tree up and get it off our vehicles." She looked up into his blue eyes and sighed. "I guess you're spending the night."

He stared at her a moment before letting a bark of laughter escape. "I never thought I'd hear those words out of your mouth again."

She shoved a lock of long brown hair behind her ear and giggled. "Yeah, I never thought I'd say them again, either. I don't see a choice, though. It's not like I can take you back to your mom's. Who would you call to come get you? Your mom is the only one who lives around here as far as I know, and Uber doesn't come to Asbury."

He kicked off his boots and plopped on the couch. "You're right. I live in Arkansas, and my sister's in Texas. The only people I know around here besides you are Mom and some old classmates I'd have no idea how to reach."

She nodded and sat next to him. "Well, I guess we may as well be civilized and talk to each other like adults. So, what do you do in Arkansas? Are you still in the copier repair business?"

He chuckled. "No. That wasn't the right career for me. I own and operate a bed and breakfast in Eureka Springs."

"I would never have pictured you doing that. What made you pursue that path?"

"Sherry and I had just divorced. I wasn't happy with my life." He studied her face as he spoke. "Copy Tech sent me to a conference in Eureka

Springs, and I saw a For Sale sign in the front lawn of the property. I was ready for a change, so I called and made an offer. That was two years ago."

"Do you enjoy it?"

He nodded. "Yeah, I really do. What about you? What do you do?"

She sighed. "I work in the office at Eagle Picher during the day and my art studio at night. My sculptures sell pretty well online and at Fancy Flamingo Flea Market in Joplin."

"You still sculpt. I should have known. I miss the smell of clay sometimes. Is that why you stay here? I was surprised to hear you're living in your aunt's old house. Is the light better here or something?"

She shook her head. "I stay here because Aunt Liz left me the house when she passed away. It wouldn't be right to sell it. There's plenty of room for me to have my studio and a guest room. My job is only twenty minutes away. The cost of living is low, and it's peaceful here."

"You mean when killer trees aren't attacking?" He grinned.

She stared into his eyes. "I'm sorry about the tree. I know being stuck here with me is the last thing you want. Hopefully my insurance company can get you a rental car so you can be on your way in the morning."

He was quiet for a moment before answering. "I'm not sorry to be here. I'd forgotten how much I enjoy hanging out with you. How your gorgeous brown eyes sparkle when you smile. How much I miss you."

She held his gaze. "I may have missed you a little, too."

He leaned closer. "What do you think about giving us another try?"

She sat back in surprise. "Devon, it's been a long time. We're different people."

He smiled. "That's why I think we can make it work this time. We're wiser."

"What about your bed and breakfast? It's over two hours away."

He toyed with a lock of her hair. "I have a manager who can handle things a few days a week. Maybe you could start selling some of your work at one of the shops in Eureka Springs. There's a bunch of art lovers there. You may find you'd want to visit often."

Whisper took a deep breath. Memories of snuggling with him in front of a fire on a cold day, walking hand-in-hand along a river bank in the sun, and laughing at stupid movies raced through her mind.

"Okay, let's try again. But, if we're going to do this, then we need to talk to each other instead of letting fear and suspicion poison our relationship."

Devon smiled. "None of that this time, I promise. I'm much better at communicating now." He leaned in and captured her lips in a slow and thorough kiss. When they pulled apart, he rested his forehead against hers. "I'm so glad we're going to be us again."

THE BIG BROWN TRUCK

BONNIE K. TESH

It was Valentine's week and the guy in the big brown truck spent more time in Grace Palmer's neighborhood every day. Willow Springs, the gated community she moved into after Christmas, catered to single women. Everyone seemed to be getting beautiful flowers and fancy packages delivered to their door. She instead, received office supplies and boxes of single-serve coffee pods, her only addiction.

This would be the first time in three years she would not be treated to a romantic dinner and a dozen red roses to celebrate the lovers' holiday. A breakup with her boyfriend, who lived in the same apartment complex as she, was painful enough without running into him with another woman's arms, decidedly younger arms, wrapped around his neck. Thus, the move.

Living in a community of women was a good choice, but there were all those love reminders delivered each day up and down the street. The rumbling of the truck could be heard when it rounded the corner, and it was hard not to miss the sound of it making each stop. She watched to see who got flowers, and she tried to guess what the plain boxes contained.

Hmm. I'll bet Ellen is getting candy. And that's probably one of those furry stuffed animals they advertised on TV at that Smith woman's door. I hate those things. Why would anyone waste their money on those? Although, I guess men think a woman would like them. Oh, and maybe that's some sexy lingerie from Victoria's Secret that Lorita is getting.

Geez. I feel like a voyeur.

Kurt, the driver of the big brown truck, was a nice guy. He was handsome in a rugged, rock climber sort of way. They had minute conversations, a few words here and there, but he rushed up to the door and was gone again in a flash.

The days her orders were to be delivered, she watched for him to stop across the street and deliver craft supplies to the woman who made her living with Etsy and E-Bay accounts.

Grace kept a coffee bar set up in the kitchen and a supply of brown throwaway hot cups with lids. If Kurt looked tired, she would churn out an expresso, but if he seemed to have some wind in his sails, it was a flavored coffee from her vast array of pods she ordered from Amazon.

A Missouri winter snowstorm made his job harder the last couple of delivery days before the big event, but the day he delivered her supplies, he took enough time to chat a bit.

"Thank you for the coffee. I really appreciate

you making it for me. You always know when I need it the most." He smiled at her.

She melted a little. "Oh, no problem. It's my pleasure. I can tell when you need a lift. Sometimes the spring in your step is not quite what it usually is." *Rats, now he knows I watch for him.* "I see you from my bedroom—my office window." *Oh dear, that's not good.* "I turned my spare bedroom into an office. I work from home."

He grinned. "Yeah, Grace. I figured. I deliver your office supplies."

She could feel heat moving from her neck into her face. "Ah, well, anytime you want a cup of coffee, honk and I'll bring one out to you."

He handed her the empty cup. "Thanks, Grace. I'll do that. Some streets are still snow-covered. It's slowed me down. Looks like I'll have to work Saturday. I don't want anyone brokenhearted because they didn't get their valentine."

She threw the cup in the trash. "I'll be here. Anytime you need a cup of coffee the coffeateria will be open."

The next day, Grace tromped out to the curb in a pair of rubber boots to retrieve an emptied garbage can. She wore her favorite work-at-home attire: sweats, a long-sleeved Henley shirt and an oversized Mackinaw sweater her brother left in her closet. The elbow was worn through. A bright orange stocking cap, a leftover from the same brother's hunting days, covered her head and ears.

Lorita, the lady down the street, stepped out on her porch wrapped in a thick wool blanket. She was the neighbor with a steady stream of suitors. Kurt delivered packages to her porch every day.

"Hey, Gracie. What are you doing for Valentine's Day, girl?" Even wrapped in the thick blanket, Gracie was a little jealous of the woman's obvious sex appeal.

The big brown truck rolled around the corner and stopped at the end of the block. She'd lost track of time. Here she stood; Gracie at her worst.

Kurt jumped out of the truck, went to the back and pulled out a package. He waved. She heard Lorita's voice loud and clear.

"Gracie? You got a date? I can fix you up."

"Don't know yet." She set the can down, twisted a strand of hair that stuck out of the stocking cap. "I have—options."

Lorita smiled, turned to go inside, then stepped back and called out. "Well, if those—options— don't work out, let me know. I got some disappointed fellas who would like a date." She chuckled. "I can't go out with everybody on one night."

Grace shook her head, turned and carried the garbage can into the garage. She chucked the boots. He could not have heard that conversation—could he? It was so—pathetic.

The next day, she heard the truck come around the corner. Kurt was running late. She was embarrassed by her appearance the day before and the conversation with Lorita. She didn't feel like looking out the window, and she would not offer him a cup of coffee.

She heard a honk. It was too much, not today. She tried to ignore it. A few minutes went by before she heard a soft knock. She waited for him to go away, then opened the door to discover a small vase with a red rose sitting on her porch. An expensive box of chocolates lay next to it. There was a note.

If you don't have plans, I would like to spend Valentine's evening with you. All the good places for dinner were booked, so if you can't go, I'll have to cancel my reservation for the window seat at the Dairy Queen. Thumbs up or thumbs down with your answer through your office-bedroom window.

Grace grabbed the gifts and scurried inside. She closed the door, stood with her back against it and laughed. She heard the engine roar to life and then another honk.

This was a special effort on Kurt's part. He spent time shopping for her with what little free time he could spare. She ran to the window, pulled up the blind and gave a definite thumbs up to the big brown truck parked across the street.

On Valentine's night, Grace brushed her long auburn hair, slipped into a stylish red dress, put on a pair of sparkly silver sneakers, and slipped the stemless red rose behind an ear. She thought it was an appropriate outfit for celebrating Valentine's evening at the Dairy Queen, with the handsome driver of the big brown truck.

About Bonnie K. Tesh

Bonnie K. Tesh is a published author whose short stories, poems, and essays have appeared in several anthologies, regional magazines, and newspapers. She is the co-author of the inspirational book, *I'll Push, You Steer; the definitive guide to stumbling through life with blinders on.* She's a member of Ozark Writers League, Joplin Writers' Guild, and Sleuths' Ink. Her critique group, The Prose Sisters, is what keeps her writing. A native of the Ozarks, she is working on a four-book series set in the Ozark Mountains of Missouri.

ICE WATER AND FIRE

LARRY WOOD

I stood at my front window anxiously watching the dreary winter sky and waiting for my husband, Jason, to get home from work. A combination of sleet, freezing rain, and tiny pellets of snow had started falling, but so far nothing had accumulated on the streets. Typical January weather in the Ozarks. Yesterday it had been sixty degrees and sunny, and now it was near the freezing mark with a winter storm brewing. If only it would hold off another couple of hours.

Jason and I planned to go out to dinner to celebrate our second wedding anniversary, and I didn't want anything to spoil it. I'd even made reservations at a fancy Greek restaurant, the same place we'd gone the night Jason asked me to marry him. We'd been back only once since. We had to watch our pennies, but I wanted tonight to be special.

I was already debating the char-grilled lobster tails versus the French onion filet when I saw

Jason's pickup turn into the driveway. Instead of stopping, though, he opened the garage door and pulled inside. I met him at the door leading off the garage into the utility room.

"Why are you parking inside? I thought we were going out?"

"We can't go out tonight," he said. "Roads are getting slick."

"They're not slick yet, are they?" I asked.

"No, but they're getting that way. The radio said to stay home unless it's an emergency."

They always say that, but I knew Jason was probably right to err on the side of caution. Still, I could scarcely hide my disappointment as I gave him a quick hug.

"Maybe tomorrow night," I muttered.

Brushing past me, he pulled out his cell phone and dialed. "Hey, Brad, Hannah and I won't be going out after all because of the weather. You wanna come over and watch the game with me?"

Suddenly, my disappointment exploded into anger. As soon as Jason hung up, I demanded, "So it's too slick to go out but not too slick for Brad to drive over here?"

"He just lives down the road," Jason argued. "That's a little different."

My eyes started watering with tears. "You didn't even remember today was our anniversary until I told you, and now you're backing out on our date. Go ahead and watch your stupid football game. That's what you wanted to do in the first place."

I strode into the living room and slumped onto the couch.

Jason followed. "Hey, I'm sorry. I know you were looking forward to tonight. Maybe we can beat the storm if we get ready and leave right now.'

"Are you sure?" I asked.

"Yeah, the roads weren't bad on the way home."

"But I made reservations for later," I remembered.

"I doubt they'll have trouble finding a table for us on a night like this," Jason said.

"Okay," I said, my tone suddenly brightening. "I can be ready in fifteen minutes."

As I dressed, I kept flashing back to when Jason and I first met. It was the fall of my freshman year at Missouri Southern, and Jason was a senior. I don't know if you'd call it "love at first sight," but it was pretty close.

Tall, dark, and handsome and president of the business club, Jason treated me like a queen. By our third or fourth date, I knew I was in love. He said he loved me, too, and I was sure he meant it.

We got married at the end of the school year, and Jason got a job as an assistant production manager. He made decent money, but he had student loans to pay back, and we both had car payments. I had to drop out of school to help make ends meet, though my job was just part-time.

Unfortunately, financial worries weren't the only strain on our marriage. Everything seemed fine between Jason and me when we first got married. We talked about our future and even talked about having a baby. Gradually, however, we seemed to drift apart.

All Jason wanted to do when he came home

from work was watch TV and go to bed. We rarely made love anymore, and I was starting to feel trapped. I wanted to go back to school, but Jason said we couldn't afford it.

Lately, I'd started feeling glad that we didn't have kids yet because I wasn't even sure I wanted to stay married. I still loved Jason, and he still said he loved me, but only if I said it first. The spark had gone out. That's why I'd been looking forward to this night, hoping our little anniversary celebration could rekindle the fire.

After hurriedly dressing, I glanced at myself in the full-length mirror on the back of our bathroom door. The blue slacks with black accessories looked good on me, and the winter boots had a high enough heel to be sexy without being impractical. I didn't consider myself beautiful, but I wasn't a slouch either. Maybe I'd gained a couple of pounds but I still looked okay, I told myself, as I put a finishing touch on my lipstick.

I met Jason in the hallway outside our bedroom, but he paid no attention.

"We need to get going." He got his coat from the closet and headed for the door.

We hardly spoke as we headed toward town. The only sounds were the pellets of snow beating on the cab of the pickup and the rhythmic swoosh of the windshield wipers. The roads were getting slick, and Jason was taking it slow, concentrating on driving. I began to feel foolish for insisting we go out on a night like this.

Coming to a low-water bridge, Jason slowed even more, but as he started across, the pickup began sliding. He tried to steer out of the slide, but the bridge was covered with a thin sheet of pure ice. The pickup went skidding off into the river and landed on the passenger's side, partially submerging me in the icy water.

I started screaming, only able to keep my head and shoulders above the water by twisting my body upward. The shock of hitting the icy water was like the polar plunge I'd taken part in a year earlier, but this one was involuntary and I was trapped inside a pickup. Frantically, I fumbled for my seat belt but couldn't get it undone.

"Help!" I yelled. "I can't get my seat belt off."

Jason freed himself from his seat belt and dropped into the frigid water beside me. Crouching, he reached into the water to try to get my seat belt unlatched but couldn't do it. Meanwhile, the water inside the cab was gradually rising.

"Get out, Jason!" My teeth chattered. "There's no use both of us drowning or freezing to death."

"No, Hannah, I love you, and I'm not leaving you. Hold on. I'll be right back."

He reached up and opened the driver's side window. Fortunately, the electronic opener still worked. Jason crawled out of the cab and started rummaging in the toolbox in the bed of the pickup. After what seemed like minutes but must have been only seconds, he was back with a knife.

Standing in the icy water, he reached down and cut my seat belt. I was shivering and confused, but somehow, he managed to get me out through the window and to solid ground, where he called 9-1-1. I started getting drowsy and numb, but Jason wrapped me in his arms and kept shaking me to keep me awake. Then I heard the distant sound of an approaching siren.

When I awoke hours later in the hospital, I could see snow falling in the daylight outside my window, and Jason was at my bedside. He'd been treated and released, but I'd been admitted, suffering from hypothermia.

"Hi." I looked up at him with a timid smile. "I'm sorry for being so foolish and causing all this."

"No," he said, "I was the one who was foolish for taking you for granted—for not appreciating you and showing you how much I love you. I was so scared I was gonna lose you."

"I love you, too, Jason." Despite my icy ordeal, a warm glow coursed through me.

"By the way," he said, "I forgot to tell you I got a raise. Maybe you can go back to school like you've been wanting."

"Maybe," I agreed, but I was really thinking that it hardly mattered at the moment.

Jason stood to leave. "I gotta go see about the truck. The doc said you'd probably be released this afternoon. I'll be back to pick you up."

When he came back to get me a few hours later, he was driving my old compact car. The pickup, he said, had been towed to the garage. The roads were still slick, but mainly just snow-covered. Not nearly as bad as the night before.

When we got home, I was surprised to see a fire already burning in the fireplace. I gave Jason a curious glance. He said he'd called in sick and had been home most of the day, except when he was at the hospital.

After we took off our coats, he escorted me to the dining room. A beautiful bouquet of red roses encircled by candelabras sat in the middle of the table. Jason lit the candles.

The table was already set for dinner with plates and silverware. The aroma of homemade meatloaf wafted in from the kitchen. Not exactly French onion filet, but I wasn't complaining. Jason had actually made dinner for me and kept it warm in the oven while he went to the hospital to pick me up.

After we'd eaten, we retired to the living room and sat on the sofa. Feeling almost guilty that Jason had gone to so much trouble on my behalf, I asked, "Do you wanna turn on the TV? Maybe there's a football game."

Jason took me in his arms. "Actually, I was thinking we might go to bed early tonight."

THE SLIPPERY ROAD TO LOVE

MARGARITE R. STEVER

"C hance, are you okay?" Daisy yelled.

The spinning tires dug into the snow left by the plows in the parking lot. Sleet pierced her skin like thousands of icy needles.

Her coworker rolled down his window. "I'm stuck in this snow drift. I knew I never should have traded my 4x4 for this tiny Honda. It's just not worth the gas mileage."

"There's no way you're getting out of that drift without a tow truck until the snow melts. Come on, I'll take you home. I'm sure you'll be able to get your car in a day or two." She ran back to her vehicle and hopped inside where it was warm.

He nodded as he rolled his window up and killed the engine. He slammed his door and stomped over to Daisy's red Chevy Impala. He slid into the passenger seat with his lips set in a firm line.

"Thanks for the lift. You're really nice to offer. You hardly even know me."

She smiled as she put her faithful car in gear. "I

know you well enough to not want you to be stranded at work all weekend. You might have that great research and development corner office, but I don't imagine the carpet would be any better for sleeping than mine in accounting."

He laughed. "No, I don't imagine it would. Thanks for the ride. I live in Hickory Hills."

Daisy furrowed her brows. "I don't know how the roads will be, but we'll give it a shot."

"If we can't make it, I can just stay at a hotel." He studied his chapped hands.

"No. If we can't make it, you can stay with me. I have a guest room." She hit a slick spot and fishtailed around a curve.

"The road is a solid sheet of ice. I didn't realize this winter storm would be so bad. We'll never make it up the hills to my place. Can you take me to a hotel on the highway?" His knuckles were white where he gripped the armrest on the door.

"In the interest of both us living through the night, I think we should go to my house." Daisy eased up to a stop sign and slid right through the intersection.

He sucked in a breath as they slid sideways toward a tree. "Okay. Yeah, your place sounds great."

"I don't live far from here. We should be able to make it. You'll like my guest room. It comes complete with clothes that will probably fit you in the closet."

"Why do you keep men's clothes in your spare closet?" He scratched his head mussing his short dark brown hair. "Wait, it's none of my business.

Never mind."

"It's not what you think. They're my brother's clothes. He's on deployment with the Navy right now. His ex-wife ran across them in a box she found in her garage when she was moving, so she brought them to me. She couldn't exactly take them to him." She shrugged. "I had space, so I washed them and hung them in the closet."

He relaxed against the seat. "Oh. That's nice of you."

Ice froze to the windshield faster than the defrosters could melt it. Daisy turned her wipers on high and continued to creep along like molasses on an ice rink.

She grinned. "Despite what you may hear to the contrary, I am a nice person."

"I don't doubt you for a minute." He grabbed the dash as another car careened toward them.

Daisy spun the wheel and they took the shoulder to avoid the other car that was sliding down the road sideways. "That was close. We're almost there." She eased back onto the road and inched her way home.

"We should have left work when they let everyone go a few hours ago. This is really dangerous." His voice was little more than a growl.

"Well, I had to finish the payroll or no one would get paid next week. With Monday being a holiday, I wouldn't have had time to get it all done before it had to be transmitted. People need their paychecks. Why did you stay?"

He snorted and shook his head. "I was running a simulation and didn't want to leave it. In hindsight,

I should have aborted the program and started fresh on Tuesday."

She pulled in the driveway of a small white house with an attached garage. She pressed the button on her visor, and they watched in silence as the garage door opened to welcome them inside.

"I'm so happy you have a garage. This ice is a killer." He relaxed his shoulders and sighed.

"I grew up in this area. I wasn't about to buy a house without a garage. Come on in and I'll make some dinner." She hit the button and the door eased closed.

She led the way into the kitchen and flicked the light switch to reveal a room that looked like sunshine. The canary yellow walls were set off with an ivy border at the top.

"Make yourself comfortable. I'll whip up dinner. Do you like spaghetti?"

He opened her refrigerator and peered inside. "Yeah, I love spaghetti. If you have stuff for a salad, I can make that while you cook the main dish."

She gazed at him for a moment with a small smile. "You'll find everything you need in the fridge." She opened the freezer and took out a pound of ground beef. She popped it in the microwave to defrost. "It should take me about half an hour to make this. You have time."

She felt him watch her as she set a pot for boiling water and a skillet for browning beef on the stove. She turned to him in question, but he averted his gaze.

He cleared his throat. "Where would I find a

knife and a cutting board to chop the veggies?" He held up tomatoes and cucumbers.

"You're quite at home in the kitchen, aren't you?"

He grinned and nodded. "It's my favorite place. I wanted to be a chef, but my father insisted I wouldn't be able to make a decent living. No culinary school for me."

She handed him the requested items. "So, you're still fairly new to the company, aren't you? What did you do before working at Duane Enterprises?"

"I was the vice president of research at Sprockets International. It was a good job, but I had to travel too much. All that time away from home makes it difficult to meet someone special." His eyes flicked to her and away.

"I see. What made you choose southwest Missouri to settle down? Do you have family here?" She transferred the ground beef from the microwave to the skillet and moved it around with a spatula as it sizzled.

"I lived here when I was a college kid and love the people. I wanted to come back to the Joplin area to settle down. I knew this was my chance when I saw the R & D manager position posted online. I applied and got hired. Here I am."

She smiled and drained the grease off the ground beef. "Lucky us."

"Yeah." He ducked his head as his cheeks turned pink.

"Am I making you uncomfortable, Chance? I promise my intentions in bringing you home with me are honorable." She grinned up at him.

He studied her for a moment. "You know, I've noticed you around the office. You have the most beautiful blue eyes. I think your dark hair really makes them pop. It's hard not to stare."

She caught her breath and could feel her face getting hot. "Oh. Thanks. I think. I'm sorry my eyes distract you."

"I'm sorry. I didn't mean to embarrass you. I like your eyes. And your smile." He sighed. "I'm screwing this up. Please forget I said anything." He turned to the counter and started chopping vegetables.

She concentrated on pouring the jar of spaghetti sauce over the ground beef and adding noodles to the water. She stirred both pots and wondered what in the world she was doing.

"Where does that leave us? Coworkers? Friends? Two people who are interested in each other?" She sighed. "I'm terrible at the dating game, which is why I'm single. I don't like dancing around this way."

His head snapped up and his brown eyes bore into hers. "Are you interested in dating me? Because if you are, you should know I'm interested, too."

Her stomach flopped as she stared into his eyes. "I'm interested, Chance."

He chuckled. "So, our first date is dinner at your place. Not a bad start."

She laughed. "Yes, but you're still sleeping in the guest room."

He nodded. "In your brother's clothes. I understand. We don't want to rush things." He ran his hand over the counter in front of him. "One question, though."

"What's that?"

He eased closer to her. "May I kiss you?"

She tilted her face toward his. "I really wish you would."

He slipped his arms around her and pulled her into the warmth of his body. He lowered his head to hers and claimed her lips with a gentle insistence that made her heart swell.

She pulled away and rested her head on his shoulder. She couldn't stop her smile if she tried. She was content to stay in his strong embrace until dinner was ready.

Later that night they cuddled on the couch with full bellies and the joy of a blossoming relationship in their hearts. As they enjoyed a rerun of an old romantic comedy on TV, Daisy smiled at Chance and said, "I never knew a snow rescue could end up so warm and happy."

ABOUT MARGARITE R. STEVER

Margarite R. Stever grew up in a tiny town of just over 200 people. She writes stories and essays that touch a person's heart. She's the 2019 President of Ozarks Writers League and a member of Joplin Writers' Guild, Missouri Writers Guild, Sleuths' Ink Mystery Writers, and Ozarks Romance Authors. She has two upcoming publications in the Joplin Writers' Guild Anthology, *Seasons of the Four States*. Her work has recently appeared in *Chicken Soup for the Soul: It's Beginning to Look a Lot Like Christmas; Anthology 2019 Sleuths' Ink Mystery Writers*; *Missouri's Emerging Writers*; *Legends: Passion Pages*; *50-Word Stories* website; the 2019, 2018, 2017, and 2016 issues of *The Crowder Quill;* the Fall 2015 issue of *The Maine Review; Mamalode Magazine's 2015 Better Together;* and *Writer's Digest 2014 Show Us Your Shorts Collection.* Her seeds of wisdom and joy can be read at ozarksmaven.com, which has been read in 54 countries.

SPRING

A BELATED MOTHER'S DAY

HOWARD FORSYTHE

It was hot that Sunday. Hotter and muggier than a typical spring day, if there is such a thing in Joplin. Our family had missed our annual Mother's Day outing of buying plants and flowers at The Botany Shop and wherever else my wife could buy colorful things to plant in our yard. She had empty pots to fill, so here we were, two Sundays *after* Mother's Day, scouring the town for shrubs and ferns and flowers and herbs and all things bright and beautiful.

We pushed carts through garden stores and pulled into our driveway with trunk loads of arboreal splendor. My wife was practically digging dirt before she got out of the car. The kids and I even helped. It was fun. It always is.

Later, after iced tea and coffee, or whatever suited us, we convoyed to an ice cream store at the Bel Aire Center at 20th and Rangeline. We sat at an outside table, chatting over chocolate sundaes and malts. It was a family thing, my wife and I, our son, two daughters, and our grandson, just being a family on our belated Mother's Day.

Rangeline traffic was heavy, but that's typical on a weekend. In the distance, we watched shoppers push loaded carts out of Academy Sports, out of Home Depot, and Walmart. A typical after-church Sunday in a town of fifty-thousand.

Our daughters eventually departed the ice creamery. My wife, son and I drove back home. The TV wasn't on, nothing to watch on a late Sunday afternoon anyway. My wife was joyfully sorting through her new flowers, but around 4:00, the skies started to cloud up.

Gray clouds. They became darker, and something in the air didn't feel right. Like an unusual tightness, a pressure beyond just hot and muggy. We had heard of a tornado watch in the area, so on came the TV and, sure enough, the Weather Channel mentioned Joplin. A belated Mother's Day celebration was about to take a nasty turn.

Tornado watches are nothing new in our town, but a tornado *warning* is something else entirely. One of the TV guys said a funnel had been spotted in the air west of Iron Gates way out on west 20th Street but it wasn't expected to cause problems. That changed. In a hurry.

It was just after 5:00 when the sirens began their ominous whine. A sound nobody likes to hear. I'd always wondered if we would know when to take cover. Is it when the sirens start that mind-numbing wail? Is it when a panicky guy on TV yells, "Take shelter!"?

Not just yet. Not for me, anyway. When all that happens, you don't instantly and obediently lockstep to your safe space. You run outside to see what's going on.

Our across-the-street neighbor was outside too. He and I stood together in the middle of 28th Street scanning an ominous dark green sky to the west. That's then we saw it.

It was far in the distance, still white, hadn't hit the ground yet to stir up its darkening cloud of debris. But it was there. And it was getting bigger. It was lowering toward the ground and it was coming toward Joplin.

He and I looked at each other in absolute horror. We knew. *That's* when you take cover!

Inside our house, it was wide-eyed chaos. Our son was on his cell phone to our eldest daughter, both nearing panic. The damn thing was just a couple miles out!

My wife, son, and I quickly gathered pillows and whatever else we hoped might shield us. We grabbed Charlie the Labrador and wedged into an interior bathroom to hunker down and pray. The sound from the wind outside grew louder. And louder. It swelled to an ugly *roar*.

When people say a tornado sounds like a freight train rumbling by, they're right. And, this time, it was *our* turn to hear the train. We were going to get hit. Our cat jumped into my lap, Charlie the Labrador was panting and scared. He was shaking like a leaf because *we* were. He knew too.

The wind picked up ferociously as the God-awful thing closed in with a loud almost deafening noise. It was on us. Then a horrible and spooky groan came from outside our closed bathroom door.

We didn't know it at the time, but a bedroom window had blown in from its frame. The wind had begun spinning our attic fan in a low-pitched macabre whine like an evil monster creeping down the hallway. Like loud sound effects in a movie theater, only this scene was real.

We clung to each other for what we thought was dear life, scared to death, yelling at the wind to *please stop!* Then, yet another sound. Like things being thrown. The loud impacts of objects hitting the outside of our house. Or, maybe objects being torn *from* our house! And all we could do was sit there, cover our heads, shudder, and wait it out. And hope to be alive when it was over.

After five minutes of almost unspeakable terror, the roar of the wind began to slow, still loud and scary, but lessening. And lessening. I took a chance and opened the bathroom door a crack.

Nothing hit me in the head, no evil monsters lurked in the hallway, but the scene outside our living room window was incredible. Shingles, torn chunks of wood and siding from peoples' homes, debris from Lord knows what had blown into our front yard and swirled down 28th Street. Twilight Zone. We worked up the courage to emerge from the bathroom, all of us shaking, hearts pounding like jackhammers. The cat and Charlie the Labrador ran down the hall and hid.

We were alive. But what about our daughters?

God, please let them be okay. *Please!*

Electric power and phone lines were out, and cell phones were sporadic. We eventually got a cell connection to our eldest daughter, whose home was undamaged, she and her husband mercifully uninjured. But no one could get through to our younger daughter.

She and her husband and our grandson lived just east of St John's Hospital. No contact and, according to our battery radio, no way to get there for all the downed trees and demolished houses blocking the streets. Sheer panic. *Please, God!*

Our eldest daughter and her husband finally made their way… on foot through rain and downed trees and power lines... to our younger daughter's house near St. John's. Much to their relief, they spotted our grandson, dazed and wandering. He led them to what used to be his home and the wonderful sight of our younger daughter and her husband alive. Alive but badly shaken. They had ridden the storm out in their basement. Their house was still standing, but that was about it.

My wife, son, and I didn't realize the full scope of what had happened. We didn't understand how lucky we had been. That sank in when I looked from our yard on 28th Street two blocks north to 26th and the sight of several demolished homes, one with a car blown onto what had once been a front porch.

A text from my boss in Springfield soon came, asking if we Joplin employees were okay. Joplin had made the news already. Then came my friends Ken and Dixie. They screeched into our driveway in wide-eyed hysteria, not knowing where to go or what to do. They stammered that their entire neighborhood near 16th and Texas had been destroyed. That's when the magnitude of what happened that Sunday afternoon really hit home.

Our house on 28th Street was damaged. Part of the roof had been blown off, but it was livable. A repair company from Pittsburg was on the way the next morning. Their trucks made their way through debris and downed trees and police barricades, eventually finding our home, covering our roof with blue plastic tarps that many other houses would soon feature.

I remember our first sight of St. John's Hospital the day after. It was from a distance, but St. John's was a haunted windowless shell. Twisted cars were piled on top of each other in the parking lots, the neighborhoods around it demolished. What had once been houses were piles of rubble with their former occupants walking the streets in a trance.

Our grandson used to speak of the giant trees in their neighborhood. For all their green leafy mass, he said you couldn't see St. John's just two blocks away. When he emerged from the shelter of their basement, the trees had been torn apart, blown into the street, and the ghost of St. John's was not only visible, it was the only thing recognizable.

I remember also our first views of the battered shell of Joplin High School, block after block of nearby houses and businesses reduced to mounds of broken timber and glass. Humbling. Numbing. Indescribable.

In the days that followed, even after the streets had been partially cleared of fallen trees and power lines, you couldn't find your way around. A house or a building that signaled a long-familiar turn into a destination wasn't there anymore. It was a pile of rubble on a concrete slab that was once its driveway. People began planting cardboard street signs on wooden stakes so you knew where the hell you were. One-third of this whole city was that way!

Iconic symbols seemed to sprout. Every driver in town was familiar with the elaborate brick sign at 20th and Indiana that spelled out Joplin High School. Most of those letters had been blown away, replaced by some blessed soul with duct tape that now spelled *Hope* High School. The iconic photo of a policeman carrying an injured child out of Walmart. The tall white cross in front of what was once St. Mary's Church on 26th Street still stands in memoriam.

The aftermath presented images forever forged. The Home Depot off Rangeline completely flattened. The nearby arches at the entry to Academy Sports looked like ruins from the Roman Empire. The battered steeple at St. Paul's United Methodist on west 26th Street, the vanished medical buildings west of St. John's.

Drivers going west on 20th Street at Connecticut once got only fleeting glimpses of the Burlington Northern trains as they crossed 20th in front of Dillon's Grocery. Now, Dillon's and the trees along the tracks were totally gone, and those trains were steadily visible all the way from 20th to the Connecticut underpass a mile away. And the Bel Aire Center on Rangeline. And its ice cream shop, where our family had feasted on chocolate sundaes an hour before the storm. Totally leveled.

But those were inanimate objects, replaceable in time. It was the *people* that stuck most in our minds. We were soon to learn that one of my co-workers and his wife had been killed, their son and daughter seriously injured, as the evil beast destroyed their house on West 26th. And a years-long friend who had been sucked through the back window of her pickup at 20th and Duquesne, seriously hurt and in a Springfield hospital for weeks after. She and her husband had just exited their son's graduation ceremony at Missouri Southern. I shudder to imagine the mass casualties if that ceremony had been held at Joplin High School just minutes earlier.

Then there were the heroes. The doctors and nurses at St. John's and Freeman who helped evacuate the sick, the police and fire departments who responded from Kansas City, St. Louis, Columbia, Tulsa, Oklahoma City, Topeka, Wichita, Fayetteville, and Lord knows where else. At practically every intersection in town, you saw a police cruiser from a far-away city flashing red and blue to help control traffic and patrol devastated neighborhoods. There were church groups and veterans who helped feed and water the unfortunate. The list was endless. And gratefully received.

Our family helped our younger daughter and our grandson. We nervously watched her husband climb to the top of their roof to nail down a blue plastic tarp to help protect their home as the rains continued. The interior of their house was a total wreck as we helped box important items on the wet floor of their kitchen. But his efforts to save their home were in vain. It was not salvageable.

As we worked that day, a pickup pulling a flatbed trailer packed with cartons of food, bottled water, and other necessities slowly inched down the street dodging fallen trees and sullen residents. We walked out to thank them for their efforts. One of them spotted my ragged work gloves and offered me a new pair. I declined, thanked him anyway, but he insisted. "Please take them, they are for you, God bless," he said. There was a look in his eyes that told me he meant every word.

Later, after the insurance settlement, our younger daughter and her husband donated the patch of land where their home once stood to Habitat for Humanity so that someone even less fortunate than they could have a home.

There were many fatalities on that wicked Sunday. One hundred sixty-one, including a Kansas City policeman who had volunteered to help our city. He was struck by lightning at 32nd and Main while directing traffic. Those fatalities are forever immortalized by parks and shrines in our community. As well they should be.

There were many hundreds injured. The people who had been hurt were delivered to Freeman and St. John's in pickup trucks and vans. Doctors and nurses did their best to triage all who were brought in.

Days later, the cleanup crews arrived. Dozens of them with huge backhoes shoveling the remains of peoples' homes into giant black open-top trailers. It seemed everywhere you went you saw one of those trailers being loaded with what used to be.

Family and friends helped clean up our own mess. We moved rain-ruined furniture to the curb. We struggled to saw and pull fallen trees out of our yard.

The debris in our yard contained nine different colors and patterns of roofing shingles, none of which were ours. They had been blown in from peoples' homes to our west. Our own shingles and roofing were in somebody else's yard somewhere.

We found something else that morning. I raked it from under a bush. It was something that made my mouth drop open. A card. A card from an old board game called "Sorry."

I picked it up in amazement. The card just simply said, "SORRY." To this very day, it remains with us and always will. We're not sure who was apologizing but, somehow, that card was meant for us. Meant for *everyone* who lived through that awful day. And for those who didn't live.

Our family was lucky. *Very* lucky. More so than many other families in and around Joplin. For that, we are forever thankful. But, also forever cognizant of those who lost so much more than we did. The horrible events of May 22, 2011, will remain eternally etched within all of us who were in Joplin on that evil day. Lest we forget. But we never will.

ABOUT HOWARD FORSYTHE

Howard Forsythe, his wife of 46 years, their three children and their grandson are long-time residents of Joplin, Missouri. His first novel, *Complicit* is available on Amazon, as will be his upcoming sequel, *Election Day.*

An avid guitarist originally from Kansas City, he was educated at the University of Kansas and enlisted afterwards. He served as a medic at Ft. Sam Houston, Texas, finishing with the Kansas Army National Guard.

Howard has served on the board of directors of two organizations and is now retired from the Joplin business world. He is a member of the Joplin Writers' Guild and can be reached at forsythehr@gmail.com.

MATRICULATION

S.V. FARNSWORTH

Longing for the parent she hardly remembered, newly promoted Captain Zinalla Yarl graduated from the Space Academy. The sun beat down and the humidity radiated up from the grass at her feet. None of her family could make it.

As soon as the gathering was dismissed, she departed through the crowds. She'd said her goodbyes this morning. Always prepared, she'd stowed her duffle bag of belongings in a footlocker at the civilian transport terminal.

Granted three days leave before she took her post aboard a star cruiser, she already had her ticket across the planet. A smile upturned her lips at the thought of Mother and a home-cooked meal. She hadn't seen her younger siblings in months. It would be so nice to sleep in her old bunk tonight.

The blare of a horn brought her up short. She was on the sidewalk near a crosswalk outside the academy. Resplendent in her dress uniform and shiny brimmed cap, she realized she'd caught the eye of a driver. He jerked his hover truck to a halt.

Four men jumped out of the cargo box on the back. There was no mistake, they were after her. Unarmed, she defended herself against the burly men until a stun pistol fired by the driver laid her out.

A broad daylight abduction was rare on Tarkish Two. That's what she kept telling herself as she groaned in pain from the blasted stunner. This shouldn't be happening.

"You'll feel better in a few minutes." A man's voice echoed in the cargo box.

"Unfortunately for you." She barely had the strength to speak let alone make him pay.

He chuckled warmly, which was odd because he'd just abducted her.

Space-black inside the cargo box, the vibrations of the hover truck beneath her back lulled her toward sleep as the agony abated. Zapped. It was actually more like sapped. Her instructors at the academy had described ways to fight the effects of a stun ray. She employed them.

In her pocket, she carried a stim tab. Since her hands were not tied, she slipped the tab into her mouth and swallowed. The effects were rapid and restorative.

"Feel better?" the man asked.

She groaned and rolled away as if she were still incapacitated.

"Don't try it. We have night vision goggles," another man said.

"Fine." She sat up, righting her mussed uniform. "What's this all about?" Being direct was usually the best.

"A job," the first man said.

She scoffed. "I have a job. Now, flip on a light. Or better yet, let me go. I have nothing you want and I certainly won't help you."

"You are what I want," the man's voice echoed in the box as the hover truck stopped.

"Well, that isn't happening." Determined to escape, she struck one of the men who held her captive.

They all joined the fight. Unfortunately, for her it was a losing battle. She failed and eventually folded under the weight of the four men.

"Feisty," the second man said beside her head.

"Would you expect less?" the first man asked.

"No, Captain." The second man's smile was apparent in his intonation.

"I'm glad you're happy. Now, get off me." This wasn't any way to celebrate four years of hard work and dedication, nor did the job sound legal, especially considering the method of hiring.

"Simmer down." A third man did not sound amused. He was probably the one she'd nailed with an elbow.

Cold metal cuffs ratcheted on her wrists and binders clamped on her ankles.

"Yell all you like. There's no point anymore," the captain said.

It hadn't occurred to her to call for help. Now she felt pretty stupid. Light flooded in when the cargo box's double doors opened, revealing the cluttered interior of a ship's hold.

"Take her to my quarters," the captain said.

She caught a glimpse of him as the men obeyed. He was the driver who'd shot her with the stunner. Twice her age.

"I'm not that kind of woman. I don't do that kind of work." She fought against the men who carried her.

"Never fear, little one. You are in no danger." The captain smiled.

"I'm not a child." She coiled and kicked the men holding her, only succeeding in getting dropped on her head.

The captain knelt and brushed her dark hair off her face. "You're my child."

Agape, she looked into his lavender eyes. "But my father is a pirate." Mother had finally confessed after years of refusing to answer.

He grinned. "One of the best. Now, come." He unlocked the cuffs and ankle binders.

She climbed to her feet, unable to take her eyes off of him. All her life she had wanted to have a father to love and be loved by. When Mother had admitted that her husband was a criminal, well, that had been difficult. Every one of her eleven siblings had his unique eyes and so did she.

"Why now?" Obviously, he'd been around often enough to create such a large family, so why hadn't he been more involved?

He had begun walking along the corridor but faced her now. "The people of our heritage are being hunted. Intergalactic legislation will pass tomorrow. It mandates the enslavement of our kind."

She scoffed. "And what kind is that?" There was only one kind, human.

"I am from a mining planet, third generation. They call it contamination but it's more than that. We, yes even you, are imbued with living crystals." His tone encouraged her to make a connection.

"Goelette Seven? What does the crystalline web have to do with...?" She began to piece it together. "The wealthy enjoy possessing power. Are you saying that they've deemed Crystalinians to be a slave class? Third generation and even fourth have no abilities to communicate mentally, let alone the data storage capabilities of a sixth-gen."

The captain laughed darkly. "Breeding stock to build their network."

A shiver ran up her spine to deaden the sensation in her limbs. "Are my siblings in danger?"

The captain nodded. "We're all slated for pickup by the authorities. The academy has your blood sample on file. I wouldn't have interfered with your life otherwise." He looked away, wiping a smudge off the metal wall.

"Interfere?" She shook her head and fought a surge of emotion that threatened to bring a flood of tears. "All my life, I've wished for you."

"I'm a wanted man." He still didn't meet her gaze, though an ironic smile contorted his face. "You've aspired to law enforcement since you were three years old."

Anger overwhelmed her emotions. "You're blaming me?"

The crewmen who had abducted her had already

backed up but now they looked away as well.

"No, little one." The deck rumbled with vibration as the ship's engines engaged, thrusting the craft off the ground. "I alone am responsible for the things I've done," he looked her straight in the eyes, "and the things I haven't done."

"I suppose you're sorry and want to be forgiven." She couldn't see how that would ever happen.

The seriousness of the moment weighed down his broad shoulders. "I am sorry and I do want to be forgiven." He took her hand and shook it. "Ben Holt, pleased to meet you."

Unmoved, she gripped his hand. "Zin Yarl, daughter of a man who has never lied before."

Shaking his head, he chuckled and pumped her hand one last time before letting go and walking along the corridor. "Come. Our family awaits in my quarters. I'll let your mother see what she can do to smooth things over with you."

Zinalla stared. "Mother's here?"

"Your siblings are here too. We're all outlaws now, little one."

SPRING OF WAR

APRIL BROCK

March of 2003 saw spring in full bloom. The bright, blue sky painted a backdrop to green trees that swayed as the wind played amongst the leaves. The flowers held their heads high, soaking in the warmth of the sun. But I sat in aching silence as a dread set into my bones. The beauty outside the window had no effect on the tension that filled our family car like dense fog.

My mind replayed the catalyst that brought me to this point. It was so fresh in my mind. It was as if part of me had remained there, doomed to relive that day over and over again.

The first period, just after 8 a.m., was American history. We were continuing our study of World War II. It was one of my favorite topics.

We sat in class watching the morning announcements broadcast when the news broke.

I'd heard all about World War II, but I'd never considered how a kid would have felt on December of 1941. I can only assume they felt like I did as I watched the impact of the second plane. You know it's bad when even the teacher is scared.

The reporter did his best to stay calm as he said, "We are under attack."

I walked right out of class, nobody noticed, all eyes were glued to the TV. I raced through the empty hallways to the payphones, dropped in my quarters, and prayed my dad would still be home.

"Specialist Bidwell." His voice was crisp and tense. The words he used were how he answered the phone when he was on National Guard duty.

"Are you deploying?" My voice came out far louder than I had meant it to. It echoed off the lockers.

"April? Are you okay? Take a deep breath and calm down. Everything is going to be all right. I haven't got *the call* yet. Mom will come to get you when it comes."

Eighteen months later, that call came. I'd have given anything for this to just be a nightmare and wake up. But I'd never had nightmares where the world looked so bright and cheery. There would be no pinching myself and waking up.

Mom drove without a word, lost in her thoughts. The tightness of her jaw said she was still mad my sister had refused to come, leaving us to face this alone. Usually, we'd be singing off-key at the top of our lungs, but today we didn't dare turn on the radio. Every DJ would be talking about what loomed ahead of us.

When we turned onto 32nd Street, I could see the US flag and the red engineer flag waving proudly at the top of the hill. My stoicism faltered as hot tears poured down my face. This couldn't be happening. I wasn't ready.

Mom parked the car and slid a tissue into my trembling hands. "Don't you dare let him see you cry. We have to be strong. He can't be worried about us." Her words fell from her lips with a tone of resignation. She was saying it to herself every bit as much as me.

I wiped my face. Together, we went inside to help him finish packing and throw his bags on the bus.

I'd come to this building at least once a month since I was four. It was like a second home. The soldiers were my family. Their families were my friends. Their boots were a lullaby of rhythm that echoed safety.

Today, I hated this building. The people in uniform were too busy to even tell me hello. Their spouses and children wouldn't look me in the eye. The sound of combat boots lashed out on the concrete like a war drum that beat in time to the pounding in my chest.

I sat on the floor next to my dad, as he showed me how to properly fold each piece of his uniform. I'd seen and done it so many times before, I could have done it blindfolded. But I listened with rapt attention and followed each instruction to the letter. I refused to fail him.

"All done." He smiled and we high-fived.

"Fall in," the first sergeant shouted.

Everyone ran to stand in perfect, straight lines. "Hooah!"

This was always my favorite part of a drill weekend. The men would be told how great they had done. Then they were dismissed to go home. *But not this time.* This time, it meant that we were nearing our final goodbye.

The first sergeant spoke. The captain spoke. Each speech was followed by a chorus of "Hooah." I paid no attention to the speeches, just my father standing tall and proud, third from the left in the second row.

"Fall out," the captain ordered, "do what you gotta do."

I think he purposely chose not to say it, but everyone knew what he meant. *Tell them goodbye.*

Dad hugged Mom, then me. He backed up and dusted non-existent dirt from his hands. "Time to go."

We could only nod as he headed to the bus. He didn't look back. I watched them file inside. I watched as they shut the door. I watched as the bus pulled away, taking my dad with it.

I was a daddy's girl, and he was gone, leaving me with just my mom. She and I barely even acknowledged the other existed. I didn't know how I could get through this. I felt so alone.

"April?"

I turned to see my mother's wet face staring at me. She had watched me and not the bus.

"Is that the last time I will ever hug him?"

She pulled me to her chest. "He can't see you now. It's okay to cry."

I clung to her with every ounce of my strength. "Are you sure?"

She pressed me against her body as her own shook. "It's the only part of any of this I'm sure of."

They say spring showers are what makes flowers grow. My tears flowed like rain and I grew stronger and closer to my mother. After all my middle name is Rose, her favorite flower.

SUMMER

IN THE FOUR STATES: SUMMER IS JUST COMING IN

GLYNN BENNION

Summer in Love
Summer in Hate
Summer in some other state
between birth's first breath
and the last gasp of death.

I love the shade of maples my father cultivated
here on Turtle line.
I love the new garden growth:
the last harvest of sweet peas,
the first ripe tomato picked at its prime
fresh from its vine,
green onions
(like frightened ostriches with their white heads
in the earth and tails in the sky),
collards both green and red
in the raised bed I spread for them.

I love white oaks and black walnut trees
 that volunteer from nuts and acorns
overlooked or lost—scattered—by that distracted squirrel
and her mate.

The various grasses grow whether I will or no
and want some herbivore or mowing boy
to keep them and the honeysuckle vines
from thinking that they own the place.
I don't own the place.
What right have they?

The hummocky ground where pigs have rooted
or moles have moiled
or men have toiled
or trucks have ground their tread into uneven earth
make of mowing a hatred
a chore to be avoided
abhorred.
So, the grasses and the honeysuckle vines survive.

I hate the welts and itchy sores—the bites of tiny carnivores:
chiggers and ticks
and helicopter mosquitoes
whose music-less hum prevents my sleep
and makes me slap my already offended ear.
I am the death of blue-black flies
that invade my living space
buzz into my beard

fondle my food.
I kill them all
with swatters
poisons
sticky strips
and even with my bare, clapped hands.
They cannot escape me.
But I am not so naive as to believe
that I can escape their patient and enduring
vengeance.
The irony is not lost on me.

The other states that I exist in make no matter.
I prefer
while I have life
to live in Love.
And though the Garden now has weeds
noxious insect pests
mice
moles
and other vermin
I love to walk in the cool of Adam's evening
in Eve's Paradise,
finding pleasure in the gifts the Father gives
from Heaven
and Good things from the Earth—my Mother
both to gladden the heart
and to nourish the soul.
To heal all wounds.
To make me whole.

About Glynn Bennion

Glynn Bennion has been involved in creative writing since childhood, writing for various school publications. In eighth grade, he collaborated with Delpha Card (sister to Orson Scott Card) to write and produce the school play, a spoof of the 1972 presidential election. Mr. Bennion studied creative writing at Brigham Young University in Provo, Utah, graduated with a degree in secondary English teaching, and has taught high school and junior high language arts for roughly the past 20 years. He writes poetry and children's stories for his 21 grandchildren and teaches language arts at Wheaton High in Wheaton, Missouri.

MARGRET

CATHERINE VALENTINE

A rhythmic sound similar to that of knuckles cracking resounded through the entryway and back into the kitchen. Margret snapped one green bean and then another. Her over-worked and wrinkled hands knew the routine all too well. *Snap.* She dropped another bean into the colander.

With bony fingers, she washed away the fertilizer, preparing the beans for canning. The sunlight through the open window above the sink revealed in the shiny surface of a pot the many crevices and age spots across a face that had been beautiful once. Now only the imagination could tell.

Like her kitchen with its yellow, greasy cabinets and cracked linoleum floor she, too, had fallen into disrepair. Her hair was once the color of dandelions, but now the gray mass was simply piled atop with a clip. She often sat alone in this kitchen and the rooms of the house throbbed with silence. The smell of pipe smoke clung to the fading curtains though the pipe no longer smoldered.

For the past week, Margret had tended the garden, washed her cup and plate, and swept the floor as a matter of course. But something was different about her now; her tired feet were less heavy and her lusterless eyes were a little clearer. Today was her birthday, but Margret had stopped celebrating those milestones years ago. No, today was the anniversary of a meeting that took place fourteen years earlier.

Each year on this day, Marian Days in Carthage, Missouri, started. Thousands of Vietnamese took the pilgrimage for the celebration to honor the Virgin Mary. On the third annual celebration of Marian Days in 1980, Margret had found herself driving through town.

Pulling off onto a side street, she got out of the truck and headed directly to a tent selling Vietnamese cuisine. They had the spicy steamed rice she loved and could never make quite as good at home. The tents were scattered about on front lawns of the town's residents—a successful peace treaty being played out.

It was Margret's 60th birthday and Billy had snubbed it as usual. In their 20 plus years of marriage, anniversaries were missed and birthdays weren't celebrated. That night in August Margret wanted something more. Love was more than just paying the bills. She wanted one special night, and if Billy wouldn't give it to her then she'd just give it to herself.

She was not the type of woman prone to rashness, but even quiet women have their moments.

She found herself standing at the door of the new dance club on Main Street and she could hear the Bee Gees' high-toned voices. Such a place was not where you would normally find Margret and that— for this night—was her plan. She tucked a strand of hair behind her ear and ducked inside. Billy never would find out where she went.

Margret had not known what to do with herself. She nervously straightened an already straight skirt. She suddenly stopped fidgeting. From across the room, she felt someone staring.

Slowly turning, her gaze fell on a handsome man with gleaming white teeth and black piercing eyes. He was obviously Vietnamese and most likely there for Marian Days. Margret spotted an empty table in the opposite corner and hurried toward it. The young man was shameless as he watched her move.

She would later learn his name was Fredrick, after his American grandfather. He really was not that young. His slick black hair and smooth brown skin made him appear more like he was in his 20s than early 40s.

Movement caught her eye as she sat and fussed with her purse buckle. Fredrick was making his way to her table. She avoided eye contact.

"You're not waiting for anyone, are you?"

Margret looked up. "No, but that doesn't mean anything. A girl can have fun on her own."

"So, she can, but why come to a dance club if you're not planning to dance?"

She didn't have a comeback and so bit her bottom lip instead.

B.T. Express's new hit single streamed across the dance floor.

"Come on!" Fredrick flashed a handsome smile that she would remember for years to come.

Margret looked at his outstretched hand and a slow smile crossed her face. She was a fair dancer—at least in the privacy of her bedroom.

"Let your hair down and let's have some fun," he said.

She put her hand in his and he easily lifted her petite frame. He rested his hand in the small of her back and gave a slight squeeze. It sent chills up her spine. He pulled her close. Close enough for her heart to thump hard, harder than it had for a long time.

Margret glanced around. No one she knew was there to see her. He was so handsome and gentle as he spoke softly in her ear. Margret knew her cheeks were flushed but she didn't care. Her feet were light on the dance floor, and they even left it as she was gently lifted on turns.

Fredrick never looked away. His eyes never wandered like Billy's always did when they spoke. She was the center of the dance floor, and in the eyes of Fredrick, she was the only one who mattered.

That was long ago but Margret remembered it well. She sat down at the kitchen table and a slow smile spread across her thin lips. She bit the bottom one. She could still hear the beat of B.T. Express and see that handsome smile of Fredrick's.

Billy had been in bed by the time she had come home that night even though it was only half-past ten. She had wondered then how long he would have waited to look for her if she had never returned, how long until he noticed the empty bed? She never told him where she had been and he never asked. That night was Margret's own.

Fingering a hairpin, she gave it a quick yank. The gray heap spilled around her shoulders. It still had body in it, even after all these years.

She usually wore her hair up, but when Marian Days came, she let it down—just for the weekend. Fredrick would look for that blond hair at the dance club on Main Street. He could always find her. In later years he looked for the gray head among the youth.

She pulled her hair around to comb it with her long fingers. Billy had never liked it down and he had never missed an opportunity to say so.

"Now Margret, what's the use of having it down? It just gets in your face, can't hardly see what you're doing."

Margret smiled, amused at the memory as she swished her hair back over her shoulder. She loved having it down now. She got up and put the colander full of green beans into the fridge. They could wait. She wanted to get out of the house for a couple of hours.

Even at 76, she had good eyes and a sharp mind. She prided herself on still being able to drive. She took off her stained flower apron and hung it on a nail in the wall. It promptly fell to the floor, ignored.

In the driveway sat a 1986 Buick LeSabre with cracking red paint and a sprinkling of rust.

Somehow this seemed fitting outside the broken-down ranch-style home that Margret locked up. She backed out of the driveway and drove west, toward town. Her thoughts centered on Fredrick and their first dance.

Marian Days were in full swing in Carthage. Ever since the initial gathering in 1978 the number of participants, not to mention the population of the town during the celebration, had grown with each passing year. Billy had never liked the traffic caused by the flood of people. Margret, on the other hand, loved to see the fresh faces. True, there was a more noticeable police presence, but seldom was there a problem.

She pulled into the parking lot of an old brick building with a brightly painted sign reading, *Not Another Darn Flea Market.* It was one of her favorite places to shop and look around. At one point in time, it had been the dance club.

The paint was peeling off the dilapidated brick walls. Buckets sat in odd places containing an inch of water from the storm the night before. Old buildings with leaky roofs were a common sight.

Margret made her way along the aisles of metal shelves full of pots and glass knick-knacks. Yellow harvest gold dishes were in plentiful supply. She ran fingers through her hair as she perused the store looking for nothing in particular.

Leaving the flea market with the bell on the door tinkling behind her, she thought of her next stop. She had one more place to go before heading home to finish the green beans. A few blocks later, she made a right turn onto a gravel road and stopped at the gate of a country cemetery.

No one was around and all was whistling wind quiet. The grinding of metal as she opened the car door put her teeth on edge. Walking between the rows, she read the tombstones: *Dorothy: Our Little Angel 11m 4 days, Rev Jimmy Lewis 1914-1990, Carol Morgan 1920-1993.* At last, she came to it, a marker reading, *Billy Dole Gardner 1918-1994.*

The grave was not yet covered with grass for it was only dug a week ago. Margret wiped her brow; the August heat was simply ruthless in this part of Missouri. She stared at the withered flowers. Not a tear was in her eyes because there was nothing left to mourn. He was gone and nothing else need be said.

She walked further along to the Williams' family plot. Stopping in front of one headstone, she stood transfixed. It read, *Fredrick Williams 1928-1993.*

Fredrick had come to Marian Days every year since the very first celebration. His family had roots in the community. His grandfather, for whom he was named, had been the police chief of Carthage back in the day and had made enemies by marrying a Vietnamese woman. His ties to that land were found in mission work in his youth. Much of the family had stayed in the community and subsequently won acceptance by joining the school board and town council.

Margret had learned all of this from her Fredrick. It became an annual practice that she would come to town and meet him at the dance club or at a local coffee shop where they would talk about anything and everything. Often, though, he would plead for her to leave her husband and go with him to Illinois where his mother's family had put down roots. But she would never leave Billy. She would never be one of those women.

At their last meeting, Fredrick had told her about the brain tumor and how she probably would not see him again. She had cried herself to sleep that night. If Billy had noticed, then he had never said a word.

Margret bit her upper lip and a tear coursed her cheek. She felt more alone now than she ever had. Fredrick was a good man. She had always felt cherished by him. Billy never made her feel like that. On their last visit, Fredrick had held her in a tight embrace and kissed her cheek. She had never allowed more, and then he left.

He died just three months before the next year's Marian Days. She'd found out from his friends. She missed him terribly. The pain had lessened over the past year, though she knew it would never go away.

As she stood by the grave, she compared the two men who had shared her life. Billy saw to her needs but Fredrick saw her. She had the strength to remember them both and the courage to be all right on her own.

About Catherine Valentine

Catherine Valentine was born in the mission field of Sao Paulo, Brazil, but grew up in Fayetteville, Arkansas. She currently lives in a tiny house in the countryside of southwest Missouri with her two cats. Catherine was homeschooled until college and earned her B.A. degree from Berea College in Kentucky after getting her A.A. degree from Crowder College. She has written two children's books, several poetry chapbooks, and a book about her first year in her tiny house. When she is not writing, she works as an in-home caregiver for special needs children.

THE MOTHER

LINDSEY HOBSON

The phone rang, and Chelsea fumbled around in her purse searching for the singing rectangle while keeping one eye on the road. Why does it always go straight to the bottom? She found it and slid her thumb across the screen.

"Hello?"

"Hey, babe, what's for dinner?" her husband asked from the other end.

"BLTs?" she suggested. "Something easy. I'm beat. We had a crazy patient-load today."

"Sounds good to me," he replied.

"Great, I'll stop at the store. We only need bacon, right?"

"And tomatoes, and bread," he replied. "Oh, and lettuce."

Chelsea laughed, "Okay, so we only need everything. Got it. See you soon." She ended the call and pulled in a parking lot.

Their five-year-old daughter, Riley, had her

seatbelt unbuckled as soon as the car came to a stop. At least someone liked grocery shopping. She let her out of the car, and together they walked through the sliding doors to start shopping.

They quickly found tomatoes and lettuce, and Riley tossed them in the basket. Then they rounded the corner from produce to meat, and Chelsea headed for the bacon. A family, consisting of a mom, dad, and adult son, were already there, and Chelsea stood behind them to wait her turn.

"How was school today?" Chelsea asked Riley as they waited. "Did you learn anything exciting?"

"We learned about planets! Did you know that Saturn has rings and Jupiter is a gassy giant? Can we get yogurt, Momma?" Riley pointed to the cooler beside them.

Chelsea laughed at her segue. "Sure, Sis. Grab a few."

By the time Riley had made a selection, the bacon was free. Chelsea grabbed a pack and headed to the checkout, picking up a loaf of bread on the way.

Once again, they found themselves behind the small family she had seen by the bacon. As usual, there was only one cashier. Chelsea sighed and shifted the heavy basket from one hand to the other.

She studied the magazine rack. The Duchess of somewhere was on almost every cover. Boring.

Her gaze drifted forward to find the son of the family in line staring intently at her. She squirmed under his gaze. The line moved slowly forward, but the man never looked away. A creepy-crawly feeling tickled the back of her neck, and she took

Riley's small hand with her free one.

It was the family's turn, and now mother and son were staring at her as the dad placed their food on the belt. They continued to stare as they sacked the groceries. Chelsea grew increasingly uncomfortable. Finally, they finished and it was her turn. Riley helped unload the basket, and Chelsea distractedly bagged it as the cashier rang it up.

Outside, she scanned all directions as they walked to the car. Riley sang a song, swinging the sack full of yogurt in one hand. Her other hand was clasped tightly in Chelsea's.

Chelsea wished she had seen which vehicle the creepy family drove. They made it to her car unscathed. She quickly opened the door to the backseat and Riley climbed in. Just as Chelsea started to put the groceries in beside her, someone shoved her from behind. She landed hard on her side and her head struck Riley's booster seat.

"Momma!" Riley shrieked.

Stunned, Chelsea struggled to sit up. Someone entered the car behind her, and at the same time someone else got in the driver's seat. She twisted enough to see the father of the family from the grocery story rifling through her purse. He handed her car keys to the son in the driver's seat, and he started the car. The whole ordeal took less than a minute and they were backing out of the parking space.

"What are you doing?" Chelsea demanded. "Where are you taking us?"

The son drove out of the lot and took a right turn, using the blinker like everything was fine.

Chelsea looked around, but there was no one chasing the car down. No one had even noticed what had happened. A drop of sweat ran between her shoulder blades and her head hurt.

The son signaled another turn and soon they were headed out of town. Chelsea noticed a van following behind. For an instant, she imagined there was a savior after all until she noticed the mother behind the wheel. The license plate on the van read, 2GAT123. She repeated the plate number in her mind like a sick nursery rhyme as they drove further from town.

The car pulled off the road and came to a stop, followed by the van. They were on a gravel road she vaguely recognized. The son and the father got out of the vehicle. Chelsea was dragged from the backseat, but to her relief they did not pull Riley from the car. Instead, the mother opened the child's door.

"Come, Dear," the mother said.

Riley got out on her own.

Chelsea attempted to slow their progress by dragging her feet. However, as she watched Riley being helped into the backseat of the van, she quickly abandoned the struggle and allowed herself to be put inside. She was buckled into the seat in the back row beside Riley who was strapped into a booster seat. It wasn't until they were moving that she finally got the answer to the question she had asked back at the grocery store.

"You'll make a fine wife for Rusty." The mother turned in her seat to face Chelsea.

"He took a liking to you at the store," the father

added. "He just knew you were the one, such a good mother."

The son, Rusty, smiled at her in the rearview mirror.

"Are you crazy?" Chelsea stared incredulously at the family in front of her. "You can't take someone because you took a *liking* to them. I have a husband. I have a family. You can't do this!"

"Now, now." The mother shook her head, anger flashing in her eyes. "That's not the right attitude at all, you sound ungrateful." She glared at Chelsea and then faced the front.

"That's enough, Mother," Rusty said from the driver's seat, "Let her be, for now. She'll come around. Give her time."

"Are you okay?" Chelsea whispered to Riley.

Riley nodded slightly but didn't say a word.

Chelsea looked around for anything in the backseat she could use to help them escape. There was trash, a sock, and a hairclip with a flower on it. The last item made her cringe. How many times had they done this?

She reached for a receipt. It was from a fast food restaurant but didn't have any information to identify the captors. Checking the pocket of her scrubs, she said a quick prayer of thanks. Usually, a pen left in her pocket meant a stain in the washer, but today it might mean salvation. She flipped the receipt over and quickly wrote *HELP!! Blue van, Kansas plate, 2GAT123* on the back.

"Riley has to use the bathroom," she blurted.

"We can't stop," said the father without a glance.

"Please, she'll have an accident in the seat."

Riley started fidgeting. "Please, can I go potty?" she said in her innocent little voice.

The mother turned around. "Oh, Roland," she pleaded with the father, "she really has to go."

Clearly, Mother had a soft spot for Riley. This might work after all. Rusty sighed and pulled into the next parking lot they passed, a gas station. Perfect. Chelsea slipped the receipt in the pocket of her daughter's jacket.

"They won't let me go with you. You have to give this paper to the person that works here. It's a secret. Do you understand?" she whispered urgently.

Riley nodded.

"I love you, Riley."

"I love you too, Momma."

"Come on, baby." Mother opened the door. "Maw-Maw will take you to the potty."

Chelsea cringed inwardly but kept her face blank. "Thank you so much," she told the smiling crazy lady that led her daughter away.

Time crawled by as Chelsea waited for her daughter to return to the van. She was acutely aware that Roland and Rusty were staring at her, but refused to meet their gaze. Finally, she saw her blonde headed child skipping out of the gas station with "Maw-Maw" in tow. Riley had a box of candy and a soda.

As soon as she was strapped in the booster seat, Chelsea whispered, "Did you do it?"

Riley nodded her head and happily ate the candy.

Chelsea relaxed slightly. The plan was weak, but it was all she had. She watched the passing cars, willing one of them to be a police cruiser. She envisioned the officer doing a double-take, realizing this was a blue van and the license plate matched the note given to the gas station clerk by a brave little girl.

"Who are you looking for?" Mother asked. "No one is coming for you."

Chelsea ignored her. Did that car have lights on top? She craned her neck to get a better view. No, it was a bike rack.

When she turned back around, she realized Mother was holding something up. It was a receipt. On it, in handwriting she barely recognized as her own, it said, *HELP!! Blue van, Kansas plates, 2GAT123*.

"I've always wanted to be a Maw-Maw," she said.

The van made a left hand turn down a long winding lane.

ABOUT LINDSEY HOBSON

Lindsey Hobson writes children's books and fictional short stories with a twist. Her first published work appears in *Seasons of the Four States*, the Joplin Writers' Guild's 2019 anthology. She graduated in 2003 from Lamar High School. Lindsey enjoys attending writing conferences and meeting local authors. She lives in southwest Missouri and can often be found hiking, canoeing, or camping with her husband and daughter.

MYSTERY MOM

ANNIE LISENBY

Ninety-eight. Ninety-nine. One hundred. Paige kicked a pebble across the sidewalk. It landed uneventfully in the grass. She glanced down the dark, lonely high school driveway then at the blank screen on her dead cell phone. She wished she was a year older and could finally drive.

If Dad's not here by the time I kick this next rock a hundred times, I'll go knock on Mr. Brown's door. Paige turned her gaze to the glow coming from the band director's window. Dad had never been this late before.

Paige found another rock and began kicking it. She lamented her predicament, abandoned in the high school parking lot. Sweat from the summer heat dripped between her shoulder blades.

At first, the idea of evening marching band practice had sounded fun. But as she counted, "Forty-one, forty-two," nothing seemed fun anymore.

A pair of headlights cut through the night, briefly drowning out the lightning bug's sporadic glow. Relief washed over Paige. The car came to a stop where she stood holding her heavy trombone case. So excited that her dad was finally here, she didn't register the slight difference in the body of the black car.

"It's about time." She pulled open the back door and tossed in the trombone. "I've been waiting for like forty minutes." When she opened the front passenger door, she froze. "Mom?"

"Get in, Paige," her mother ordered as she glanced in the rearview mirror.

Paige blinked and pushed her heavy glasses back up her nose. "You're supposed to be in Europe," she sputtered through shock.

"I'm back. Now, get in, honey," her mom commanded.

"But Dad?"

"I'm going to take you to Dad. Please, I need you to get in the car."

Paige's mom leaned across the seat, holding out her hand. She looked the same as she had the day she left for an overseas job when Paige was in eighth grade. Alice still had the same light blonde hair tied back in a ponytail, and although her brown eyes were the same color, tonight they betrayed a panic oozing from within.

"Mom, I haven't seen you in two years. Don't you get that? You left. You abandoned us." Paige stepped backward and crossed her arms. "I'm waiting for Dad."

"Look, I'm sorry. I'll explain everything. But I

need you to come with me now!"

"No. You can't come back and start telling me what to do. I'm waiting for Dad."

Another pair of headlights cut across the night. When Paige turned to look for her dad's car, Alice grabbed her arm and yanked her forcefully into the vehicle. The door still hung open and Paige's feet flailed in the night air. Her screams joined the squeal of the tires on the hot pavement as she and her mom sped away.

"Mom! Stop!" Paige clung to her mom's arm. "I'm not in the car!"

Her mom wasn't behaving like the person who had disappeared two years ago. Alice had been the typical soccer mom and accountant, the kind that limited how much sugar Paige ate and insisted she take music lessons even when she complained about them endlessly. This Alice drove like a NASCAR expert, weaving around a truck and turning abruptly down a side street. The benefit of the sharp turn was that the force thrust Paige toward her mom hard enough that she was able to pull her feet into the car as the door slammed shut with a crash.

"Put your seatbelt on," Alice said curtly as she glanced again in the rearview mirror.

"Mom, you're driving like a maniac." Paige fought with the seatbelt. "Where's Dad?"

"Your dad was kidnapped." Alice replied.

"What?" Paige braced herself as Alice screeched through another turn onto a dark street. "Who kidnapped him?"

"I did."

"What? Why?" Paige screamed in disbelief.

Guilt was written all over Alice's face. "I had to. It was for his own safety. We'll get him now. I just need your necklace, the Lego brick one I gave you for your birthday."

"That thing? I don't know where it is."

"Your dad said you wear it every day. We need that necklace." Alice punctuated her insistence by turning the car sharply, slamming the breaks, and bringing the car to an abrupt stop at the curb in front of an eerie looking park.

"I don't have to do anything for you. I haven't heard from you in two years, Mom! I don't owe you anything." Paige reached to unclip her seatbelt.

"I didn't want to leave, Peanut. I had to. There are some things I can't fully explain now. But I need that necklace to save your dad and then I'll be gone again." Alice deflated, her head dropping to rest on the steering wheel. "I made a mistake. I need to fix it, and I can't unless I have that necklace."

"Mom, what's going on?" Paige's anger abated after seeing her mother's desperation.

Alice sat up again and straightened her shirt. "I shouldn't be telling you this, but I'm not an accountant. Sweetheart, I'm a spy. I've been a spy since before you were born."

Paige didn't move, allowing Alice's honesty settle around them. "Does Dad know?"

"Yes, he knows. That's why we left the necklace with you. It has a hidden flash drive, and some very bad people are looking for it. I took your dad to keep him safe until I could get the necklace. Paige, I need your help."

Suddenly, Alice looked older than Paige

remembered. The creases around her eyes were deeper and her lips were pressed tightly. Alice was telling the truth; Paige knew for sure.

"It's in my old playhouse with my Barbies."

Silently, Alice and Paige rode through the dark streets. Paige stared blankly out the window, and Alice only moved to regularly check the rearview mirror. Luckily, no one seemed to be following them. They arrived at the green house with the blue front door, the door Alice had painted because it was Paige's favorite color.

"Stay close to me, and if anything goes wrong, either take cover or run as fast as you can, okay?" Alice pulled a gun from an ankle holster under her pant leg.

"Is that really necessary?" Paige asked, aghast.

"Bad people, Paige. Really bad people." Alice slid out of the car.

Paige reluctantly followed her, trying to cover her fear with teenage angst. In the backyard, Alice looked around systematically as they crossed to the old playhouse Paige's dad had built. Alice went straight to the big pink plastic bin, tore off the lid, and dug through it.

"Where is it?" Panic intensified in Alice's voice.

Paige began to worry. "Mom, how bad are these people?"

"Remember that scary movie you watched at Amy's sleepover in fourth grade?"

"Yeah, I had nightmares for a week."

Alice stopped and looked Paige directly in the eyes. "Multiply that by a hundred. Now, where's the necklace?"

The sound of rustling in the bushes snapped Alice's attention to one of the lace-fringed windows. She held her gun ready to fire. Paige plunged her hand into the bin and pulled out the blue Lego block necklace.

"Got it." She dropped it around her neck.

"Let's go." Alice led Paige back to the car with the gun poised and ready for action. They jumped in and sped away.

Paige knew the streets well, ones she'd explored on her bike every day after school. She noticed the houses of friends and neighbors, mentally saying their names as they passed. It was a soothing exercise after the chaos of the last fifteen minutes. Alice whipped the car into Mrs. Berger's driveway. The "For Sale" sign in the front yard reminded Paige that she had moved into a nursing home last month.

"Come on." Alice slipped from the car with the gun locked in her hands.

Paige followed close behind, her pulse pounding in her ears. At the front door, Alice holstered the gun and used an app on her phone to unlock the realtor's lockbox. Alice swiftly removed the house key, opened the front door, and pulled Paige inside.

"He's in here," she said in the dark living room.

Paige followed Alice closely, trying to match her stealth. In the back of the house, Alice pushed open a door to a bathroom and stopped short. She didn't move, not even to breathe. Dread and panic poured from Alice, flooding the empty spaces in the room.

"Oh, no," she whispered. "We have to go, now." She grabbed Paige's arm and dragged her back through the house.

They rushed to the car. As Paige opened the door, she heard a ping from her mom's phone. Alice looked at the screen. From across the hood of the car, Paige couldn't read the message, but she could read the emotions that ran across Alice's face. Confusion. Realization. Terror.

"Get in and buckle up. It's going to be a long night, kiddo."

ABOUT ANNIE LISENBY

An Ozarks native, **Annie Lisenby** has traveled the country and overseas. After studying theatre in college and graduate school, Annie worked in live theatre and the film industry. She is currently teaching theatre at Crowder College as she pursues writing. Annie has been published and won awards from the Joplin Writers' Guild, the Ozarks Writers League, and The Crowder Quill.

A HUNGER FOR LIFE

BILLIE HOLLADAY SKELLEY

Chloe and I are sitting on the bus waiting.

"What are you looking for, Lily?"

"I'm looking for Granger, but I don't see him."

Granger is one of the Ge. He takes care of us in the meadow. He helped us get on the bus this morning, but I cannot see him now.

The bus starts, and we move away from the meadow.

When the Ge landed on Earth two years ago, there was so much confusion and fear. Chloe and I were only seven then, and we were sad because our parents were taken away. There was no food, and we got so hungry. Chloe got really sick, too. It was a terrible time, but then Granger came and took us to our new home in the meadow. He has brought other kids, just like us, to live there, too. Since Granger came to care for us, we have been fine.

"Look out the window at all the crops in the

fields. Is that lettuce, Lily?"

"I don't know. Whatever it is, there sure is a lot of it."

In our meadow, we eat when we want. We play games on the grass and swim in the lake. We don't go to school. We just have fun. Granger is our doctor. He feeds us and keeps us healthy. I remember our old doctor. He gave us shots with a sharp needle. My arm hurt for days! Granger never hurts us. He gives us vaccines, but he uses little patches that look like tape with small points on one side. He just sticks them on our arms, and they melt right into our skin.

"Chloe, do you remember our old doctor giving us shots with a needle?"

"No," Chloe answers. "I don't remember."

Chloe doesn't remember as much as I do. Granger says it is because she was ill for so long. He thinks with time, Chloe's memory will improve, and she will remember more.

Granger is a good doctor. He checks our blood to be sure we're getting enough vitamins and nutrients. He uses a little ball that he puts on our skin. He says it uses a vacuum to suction blood from our capillaries, but it doesn't hurt. You don't even bleed. Granger says Chloe and I are good at making the most out of the least ingredients. He says we are efficient.

"There are only twelve kids on the bus. Why didn't they let the little kids come on the trip?" Chloe asks me.

"I heard Granger say anyone above 40 kilograms could go. I guess the little kids were too small. Do you remember when we went to the amusement park with Mother and Father? For some of the rides, you had to be so tall and weigh so much. Remember?"

"Not really. Do you think we are going to an amusement park now?"

"I don't know. I hope so."

A girl with blond hair turns toward us from the seat across the aisle.

"I'm Bridget. Do you know where we are going?"

"No," Chloe answers. "Do you?"

"I have no idea," Bridget says. "You two are identical twins, right?"

"Yes," I answer. "I'm Lily, and this is my sister, Chloe."

"I have a fraternal twin," Bridget says softly. "My brother. His name is Paul."

"Is Paul on the bus?" I ask.

"No. He got moved to another meadow. Paul is really smart. I think Granger got tired of Paul asking him so many questions."

"What did Paul want to know?"

"Oh, just little things, like how come all the Ge can speak English."

"What did Granger tell him?"

"He said the Ge speak many languages … and that speaking and understanding a language makes it easier for them to work in a new place. The Ge are farmers. Something bad happened to their planet, and they couldn't grow food anymore. That is why they came here. We have good soil."

"Oh." I think for a minute about what Bridget

has said. I wouldn't want Chloe sent away. I wonder about Paul, so I say, "What else did Paul ask?"

"He asked how many planets the Ge had taken over and how many Ge there were. Things like that. He found out that the Ge are experts at cloning."

"What's cloning?"

"I'm not exactly sure, but Paul explained it like this. He said if the Ge find one thing they really like, they can make a zillion copies of it. Do you remember all the crops we saw earlier? The Ge grow them. That's how they are able to feed all of us."

A boy with red hair, sitting in the seat behind us, interrupts our conversation. "You girls don't know anything. It's not just crops the Ge clone. They clone people, too. They like meat with their vegetables ... and they especially like veal. If Paul was sent away, he was sent away to be eaten."

Bridget gasps loudly and turns white. Chloe shudders beside me. I don't know what veal is, but this boy is mean and rude. He's scaring Chloe and Bridget.

"That's a terrible thing to say," I tell him. "The Ge are nice. They take care of us."

"Right," he nods. "They're great. They fatten us up in the meadows like cattle and keep us healthy. Then, when we're big enough, they take us to be processed for their food. I know. I used to live on a farm. I've seen what happens to the cows we used to eat, and the Ge adopt our practices. They take you to a slaughterhouse, restrain you in a chute, and fire a metal bolt into your head."

I turn away from this mean boy. Chloe is crying. Bridget has slumped back in her seat.

"If you have any brains," the boy continues, "when this Ge bus driver stops, you better run for your lives."

We turn off the road and enter a large parking lot. I hear music. It's coming from a huge building on the other side of the lot. I hope it's an amusement park.

The Ge bus driver tells us to exit in a single file and to queue up in the roped-off lanes that lead toward the building. I enter the closest lane, but the other kids suddenly bolt. They run in all directions. The Ge bus driver chases a small boy with freckles, but the boy runs fast. I see the boy with red hair running toward the woods. Chloe and Bridget are right behind him. I yell at Chloe to stop, but she doesn't hear me. She is already far away.

I consider following them, but I really want to go to an amusement park. These roped-off lanes look just like the wait lines at the park we visited. I had cotton candy. It was so much fun.

I take a few steps forward, but then I turn and look for Chloe. Everyone, including the Ge bus driver, is out of sight. I wish Chloe would have stayed with me.

I walk in the roped lane one way till it turns and switchbacks in the other direction. It repeats several times, but with each step, I am closer to the entrance.

I reach the door and look around before opening it. No one is there. All the kids have run away, and the Ge bus driver has gone after them.

Slowly, I open the door and tiptoe inside. It's dark and cold. I'm on a concrete deck, but I can still hear music. Far below me, I see a large, illuminated room. There is some type of noisy, churning machine beneath me. Beyond it, a Ge commander is giving orders to dozens of Ge workers. They are busy cutting things on a long table. I lean forward for a better look. The workers' hands are red. It looks like their hands are covered in blood.

I'm suddenly afraid. Could that boy with the red hair have been right? I feel sick. I think I'm going to throw up. I must leave. I take a step back toward the door.

Someone grabs me and puts a hand over my mouth. As I try to pull away, I see it is my father! He motions for me to be quiet, and then he whispers.

"Lily, I've been waiting so long for you. I knew one day I'd find you."

I hug my father. I'm crying, but I am happy.

"Lily," he whispers. "A few of us have escaped. We've formed a resistance group, and we're fighting back against the invasion. I'll explain later, but we must go before they see us. We're in danger just being here."

"What about Chloe? We have to find Chloe."

"Chloe? She's gone, Lily. Remember? She got sick and died right after the Ge arrived."

My cheeks are hot. The room is spinning. I feel so dizzy.

"No," I shout. "She was with me on the bus. Chloe's been with me for the past two years."

"Don't yell, Lily. They'll hear us. That girl is

just another clone. They've made so many."

"No," I shout even louder. "Chloe is outside. I just saw her. She's outside."

I hear footsteps. Two Ge workers appear on the deck. They grab my father. The Ge commander is right behind them, and he gives another order.

"Mince the bull. Obtain regulatory DNA samples from the calf and process the remains."

The Ge workers push my father off the deck. I lean over to try and see where he went, but all I can make out is the big machine churning below. One of the Ge workers grabs me. The other one is holding something that looks like a gun. He places it on my forehead right between my eyes. It feels cold. I hear a loud swish. I can't see.

AUTUMN

OFF THE GRID

LARRY WOOD

I was sitting in my easy chair reading *Backwoods Home Magazine* by candlelight when Old Rex started barking outside. "Hey, what's going on out there," I yelled.

Probably just some wild critter, I figured, but the barking didn't stop. Instead, it rose to a deep-throated howl, and then I was startled by a knock on the door. *What the hell?* Who could be coming to our shack after dark on a chilly, fall evening?

The "No Trespassing" signs were usually enough to keep nosy folks at a distance, and if the signs didn't do the trick, the dog almost always did. Rex wouldn't actually bite anybody, but he could sure make you think he was going to.

I glanced at the open bedroom door as I got up from my easy chair to investigate the unwelcome intrusion. "Nothing to fret about, Mama. I'll take care of it."

Grabbing the twelve-gauge shotgun that leaned

against the wall near the old wood stove, I strode to the door and peeked through the blinds. In the dim moonlight, I saw three or four teenaged boys standing on and near the steps, laughing and carrying on. *Must be Halloween*, I realized, although I didn't keep track of the days.

"Damned pranksters," I said under my breath.

"Trick or treat!" the boys guffawed almost in unison as I flung the door open, but then they saw the shotgun. Their wide eyes shone in the glow of the moonlight, and they turned to run like scared rabbits as I raised the barrel toward the sky.

"Get the hell out of here," I yelled, "and don't come back."

Old Rex took off after them barking at their heels, and when they were fifty feet away, I fired a warning shot into the sky above their heads. The boys raced down our dirt lane as fast as they could go toward the road a quarter mile away, where they'd no doubt left their car.

I whistled at Rex and hollered for him to come on back, and the dog came trotting toward me beneath the autumn moon. "Good boy," I said, as I turned and started into the house.

After putting the shotgun in its place, I walked toward the bedroom and paused in the doorway. "It's okay now, Mama," I said. "I don't think them boys will be around again."

Mama didn't wake up, though. She'd always been a heavy sleeper.

But the nighttime interruption had rattled me, and I needed something to settle my nerves. Back in the combination kitchen/front room, I poured a shot of Jim Beam and settled down on the couch, where I usually slept.

Hardly anybody ever came to our little house in the woods, and that's the way I liked it. Ten years ago, after I got hurt at the factory, I took disability, and we moved out here—away from town, away from civilization, away from the rat race. Just me and Mama. We liked being alone. At least I did, and Mama never complained.

We liked being self-sufficient—growing and preserving our own food, making our own clothes, and such as that. I did most of the outside work, and Mama took care of things indoors. I mowed the grass, and she did the housecleaning. I grew the green beans, and she canned them. At least that's how things worked until this past summer when Mama got sick and took to her bed. Since then, I'd kinda let things go, because I was spending most of my time taking care of her.

The first shot of whiskey didn't take the edge off; so, I poured another one. Then another. I'd lost track by the time I started feeling drowsy and lay my head down on the couch to rest.

The next thing I knew, the morning sun was shining through the flimsy, floral curtains in the front room. I got up and went outside to the outhouse and then came back in to check on Mama. She was still lying in bed; so, I kissed her on the forehead and left her alone.

I was just getting ready to go back out and fetch some firewood when old Rex started barking again. I peeked out the window and saw a car coming slowly down our lane. From the red light on top, I knew it was a lawman's car of some sort, even though the light wasn't flashing, and no siren was sounding.

The car stopped about a hundred feet from the house, and I saw two men in the vehicle. Rex ran out and challenged them, growling and barking as he raced back and forth in front of the car. When the two men got out, I recognized the driver as Jerry Goddard, a guy I'd gone to high school with in the nineties. I'd heard he was a McDonald County deputy, but this was the first time I'd seen him in years. I opened the door and walked out onto the front steps to greet him and his partner.

"Get over here, Rex," I yelled.

The dog barked a couple of more times, but, when I yelled at him a second time in a harsher voice, he started whimpering and retreating from the lawmen.

I nodded a greeting when the deputies approached, and they paused a few feet from the steps. "What can I do for you, Jerry?"

"We got a complaint you fired a shot at some boys last night," Goddard said. "Is that right, June?"

I had the same name as my old man, and I'd gone by Junior as a kid. Dad died when I was just eight, and I started going by Isaac in sixth grade. Mama was the only person who still called me June. Anybody else who did was just being mean. So, right off the bat, I was in no mood to cooperate.

"What if I did fire a shot?" I challenged in answer to Goddard's question.

"It's against the law to shoot at people, Hoffman," Goddard said, switching to my surname.

"I didn't shoot at nobody. Just shot above their heads to scare 'em off. They were trespassing and disregarding the signs I got posted."

The other deputy, whose name tag said "Joshua Rivers," chimed in, "Be that as it may, we can't have you shooting at people for no good reason."

Rivers looked as if he couldn't have been over twenty-one years old, but here he was telling me what I could and couldn't do. "I had a good reason," I said. "Those boys were scaring Mama."

"How is your mom?" Goddard asked.

Why would you care? I thought. *You never liked my mama any better than you liked me.* But I didn't say what I was thinking. Instead, I answered his stupid question. "Mama's sick in bed, and those boys were scaring her."

"Those boys just came out here on a Halloween dare," the kid deputy explained. "They didn't mean no harm."

"I didn't know that. I thought they were trying to break in. Last I knew, Missouri was a stand-your-ground state."

"Well, that's not the only reason we're out here," Goddard persisted. "Those boys also reported that they smelled an awful odor coming from your house when you opened the door."

"Is it against the law nowadays to have a stinky house?"

"Depends on what's causing the stink?" the kid deputy said.

"What's that supposed to mean?" I asked.

"Do you mind if we come in, Isaac?" Goddard asked, using the name I preferred.

Trying to get on my good side, but I wasn't falling for it. "You got a warrant?"

"No, but we can get one. Why don't you just save us the trouble?"

I snorted at the suggestion at first but then gave a shrug. "Hell, why not? I got nothing to hide. Come on in."

I swung open the door and invited the lawmen inside with a sweep of my hand. They stepped onto the landing and brushed past me. As soon as they walked inside, they started gagging and covering their mouths like they could hardly breathe. I knew my place didn't smell like a flower garden, but it wasn't as bad as they were letting on.

While the deputies paused just inside the front room, I stepped to the bedroom doorway and glanced inside. "There's some deputies here who wanna look around, Mama."

She was still asleep and gave no sign of hearing me. So, I stepped into her room and spoke in a louder voice. "It's about those kids that were bothering us last night, but it's nothing to worry about."

When Goddard walked into Mama's room, I retreated to the doorway, where Rivers and I stood side by side. "How can you stand it in here?" the kid deputy asked between coughs. "It smells like something's dead in here."

Goddard hovered over Mama's bed and touched her brow. "Oh, my God!" he exclaimed, as he turned and staggered back out of the room, nearly knocking me and the kid down. Glancing from me to his partner, Goddard's face wrenched with horror. "There is something dead in there, Josh," he said "That old woman's been gone for no tellin' how long."

ABOUT LARRY WOOD

Larry Wood is a retired public-school teacher and a freelance writer specializing in local and regional history. He has published two historical novels, eighteen nonfiction history books, and approximately 500 magazine stories and articles. His books can be viewed at his Amazon Author Page, https://www.amazon.com/Larry-Wood/e/B001JS47RE/ref=dp_byline-cont-book-1. He has also contributed short stories to several anthologies, including the popular *Mysteries of the Ozarks* series.

Wood has won numerous writing awards from organizations like the Missouri Writers Guild, the Ozarks Writers League, and the Ozark Creative Writers, Inc. In 2011, he received the Walter Williams Award, given by the Missouri Writers' Guild for best major work, and he has also won the same organization's Best Book about Missouri award four times. In 2016, he was named an honorary lifetime member of the Missouri Writers Guild. Wood taught a correspondence course in nonfiction writing for the Long Ridge Writers Group for eighteen years, he is a former staff writer for *Show Me the Ozarks Magazine*, and he maintains a blog on Missouri and Ozarks history at www.ozarks-history.blogspot.com.

STREET DANCE

MARJORIE WOOD

Mulberry's annual fall street dance was held on the night of the full moon in the month of October. Invitations were sent out a week before the dance. Like the rest of the uninvited town folks, Lucy stood at the barriers to catch a glimpse of the happenings. All she could see were flashes of lights and hear the muffled music. Like everyone else in town, she wondered why the dance was by invitation only. The invited would be asked after the dance but no one talked. They just walked away in an exhausted daze.

Each year, since she was a little girl, she would run down to the mailbox to check for an invitation. Today she dropped all the mail except the square envelope. Her hands trembled as she carefully opened it. She pulled out the thick card and read the gold-lettered invitation. Letting out a squeal, she held the card to her chest. This year she was one of the lucky few to get an invitation.

She dashed back to the house and sorted through the few dresses in her small closet. Not an appropriate one to wear. On her way out of the house, she grabbed her purse. She only had seven days to find the best dress for the dance. She didn't want to disappoint the hosts. They needed to know she was not a country hick.

After an exhausting search of several shops in the Four States, she started to panic, not a single suitable dress. With one day left, she drove to Kansas City. There just had to be a perfect dress there. She parked her beat-up white pickup truck in front of Camille La Vie. Squinting, she checked the time they opened, and with a sigh, she sat back. Having two hours to wait, she watched the dark sky change from black to a blaze of orange and red, then to pale blue before someone came to unlock the door.

She jumped out of her truck and marched across the parking lot. She had to smile at the startled look on the store clerk's face. Emergencies called for drastic measures, and that included driving more than two hours in the dark to a fancy-dress shop. Maybe the small-town dance in Mulberry wasn't an actual emergency, but she wanted to be the best-dressed person there.

"Excuse me." Lucy forced the lady store clerk back against the wall.

Stopping for a few moments, she looked around the cozy shop. To her right was the register with shelves of perfume behind it. The shelving continued around and extended to the ceiling filled with a rainbow of slacks and blouses, none of which she wanted. But, in the center of the store were racks of what she came for, beautiful dresses.

It took all she had not to yell, 'Woo-hoo!' and stomp her feet. Instead, she did her best to glide over to the dresses. All she managed was a clip-clop sound in her dirt-caked cowboy boots. She glanced back at the clerk and thought about neighing like a horse, but changed her mind after seeing the glare sent her way. Perhaps shoving her into the wall had not been the best thing.

Lucy ran her hand across the dresses; so many to choose from. She checked the price and clenched her teeth, $375.00. She didn't have near enough. Maybe they had something on sale. She tried to look around for the clearance rack without the clerk taking notice.

All she saw were rack after rack of expensive dresses. With a heavy sigh, she slowly turned toward the door. Just then, out of the corner of her eye, she spotted the small clearance sign.

With a slight smile, she grabbed a couple of dresses off the regular priced rack in front of her. She strolled around and casually pulled out items, looked at them, and then put them back until she made it to the reduced-price dresses. She checked, and with relief found they were marked down to her price range.

Sorting through the clothes, she rejected them one at a time for not being her size or style. Toward the end of the rack her throat tightened. She would have to slink out without a dress. She ripped the last one off the rack, and with hands trembling she checked the size. With relief, it was her size. The white, multicolored polka dot dress was perfect.

She marched across the room with the three dresses toward the clerk. "I would like to try these on."

The clerk sneered at her as she picked up the keys. "This way." She walked around the register.

They walked to the back of the store. The clerk unlocked the door and stepped aside. "Just so you know there is no back door." She smiled at Lucy.

Lucy smiled back. "That's good to know in case of a fire." She pointed her nose into the air and walked into the fitting room.

She hung the two unwanted dresses on the hook. Pulling on the white dress, she smiled at the feel of the material. It felt expensive. She turned to the side and back around to the other side as she checked herself in the mirror.

Smiling, she spun around to make the dress flare out. Perfect was all she could think. She held her breath as she checked the price. $450.00 regular price, marked down to $175.00. She let out the breath she'd been holding. Even the price was perfect.

Returning to the clerk, she handed the other two dresses to her. "I don't want these." She laid the white polka dot dress on the counter. "I will take this one."

Lucy returned home dreaming about what the night of the dance would be like, and all the compliments she would get for being the best dressed there. She anticipated with delight the dancing, singing, and socializing that would happen until, in a daze, everyone left in the morning.

The night of the dance, Lucy's hands shook as she tried for the third time to put on her earrings. She leaned on her vanity and took a deep breath. Letting it out slowly, she thought this was silly, she knew all these people. She'd lived here all her life and knew most of the 200 people that lived in Mulberry. With another try, she was able to slip the silver teardrop earrings into her ear lobes. One last fluff of her brown curly hair, a close check of her make-up in the mirror, and she deemed herself perfect.

She walked a couple of blocks to the barricades. Already, there was a line of about ten people to get into the dance. A large man with slicked back, black hair had been checking for invitations and now had a small man lifted off the ground.

Mr. Slicked Hair tossed Mr. Small to the side and yelled. "No invitation, no entry."

Lucy snapped open her white purse and checked for the gold-lettered card. She stepped behind the last person with a satisfied smile that she had her ticket into the dance. A few minutes later she slipped the card out and handed it to Mr. Slick.

Mr. Slick took the card. "Welcome, Miss Lucy Schultz. Enjoy the night."

She flounced through the gate and walked the block to the street dance area. Her mouth fell open at the lack of decorations. A few strings of twinkle lights were strung across the street. No dance floor at all.

Three orange and black striped trash barrels were set out, and a couple of tables filled with home-cooked food set on the right side of the street. On the left side, a disc jockey was set-up on a trailer with a few colored lights. There should be more, considering all the hoopla about the dance.

Why did people leave in a daze? She thought about leaving but changed her mind when Billy Smith smiled at her from the other side of the street. With a glance around, she knew she was the best-dressed lady here.

The sunlight faded into night, and the twinkle of lights came on, washing the area in colors of red, yellow, green, and blue. The music started, and everyone gathered in the middle of the street to dance. Lucy joined the dancers by herself for a few moments before Billy made her his partner.

Hours later and ready to drop, Lucy stopped to take a break. She noticed several people dressed in black whom she had never seen before. They encircled the dancers and just stood there watching. What were they waiting for? Why didn't they join the dancing?

Suddenly, the strangers darted into the crowd, grabbing the person closest to them. The dancers screamed and raced from the strangers. With no chance of escape, the dancers were shoved to the ground with the strangers on top.

Lucy turned to run but Billy grabbed her. "Where do you think you are going?"

"What's happening?"

"The same thing that happens every year." Billy bared his fangs. "We feed on the people of this town. Mulberry's tradition of a street dance gets people together in one place."

He slid his finger down her cheek. She jerked her

face away from him and saw the strangers biting the town folks' necks, feeding on them. In a moment, she would be joining them. She closed her eyes, all that time wasted finding the perfect dress only to become a vampire's dinner.

How could this be? No men and women elegantly dressed whirling around the dance floor waltzing to the music. No right moments for lovers to glide off the dance floor and share a kiss. She wouldn't ever have that right moment. Her fantasies of romantic grandeur shattered. All she got was a blood bath.

Billy leaned down to whisper into her ear. "I will make you my bride."

She smiled. Billy bit. She screamed as the searing pain burned through her body changing her. Starved for blood, she and Billy joined the rest of the vampires.

At least part of her dreams of the street dance had come true. She had met someone with whom she would spend the rest of her life. Correction. The rest of her afterlife.

ABOUT MARJORIE WOOD

Marjorie Wood has been a member of the Joplin Writers' Guild since 2016. She writes thriller and mystery stories and is currently working on her first mystery book. She has a bachelor's degree in commercial graphics and likes to paint. She enjoys spending her free time with her Yorkie babies and crocheting. For the last seventeen years, Marjorie has worked in Joplin in payroll for a large trucking company that delivers new trucks. Marjorie was born in Kansas City, Kansas, and has always lived in southeast Kansas, finally settling in a small town of 500 people.

NEIGHBORHOOD HALLOWEEN

MICHAEL GRAHAM

It was Halloween and I'd just opened a bag of candy on my front porch. I took a seat on one of my lawn chairs as the sun set and waited for the kids in costumes. I looked to the east and west of my street, seeing kids starting to come from both ends.

As I waited, I saw Old Man Hawkins across the street sitting on his front porch. He was dressed as a scarecrow and being very still as he waited for kids to scare, just as he did every year. He was a widower and loved scaring the teens.

I always enjoyed watching the teens run in fear. Old Man Hawkins told me last year that he hadn't even given away any candy to the teens, because they had all run away scared. We had a pretty good laugh at that.

I saw the first group of kids making their way to my house. As they approached, I stood up and walked to my top steps and held out the bag of candy.

"Happy Halloween," I said. "Come get you one piece."

The kids walked up and one by one they took candy from me. There were three young kids all dressed up. The youngest was a cowboy, the little girl was a princess, and the oldest boy was a ninja. They walked across the street to the waving scarecrow to get more candy. It was nice to see the young kids wave to the nice scarecrow.

As I looked for more kids, I saw teens walking up without any parents.

"It's show time, " I said to myself.

Old Man Hawkins had the same idea, as he went very still and waited. The teens came running up to me, not even in costumes, but only in face paint. I handed each one a piece of candy and smiled. I knew it was trick or treat time.

They ran up to Old Man Hawkins' house, looking for candy, and spotted a bowl of it beside the scarecrow. As I watched, excitement rose up in me.

The teens walked over and the scarecrow jumped up all of a sudden. The teens jumped back, and each of them screamed so loud it echoed through the neighborhood. They took off running. One stumbled on the steps as they ran as fast as they could out of sight.

I laughed so hard, but not as hard as Old Man Hawkins. He doubled over with laughter, and slapped his leg. He looked up and noticed me laughing as well and gave me a wave. I waved back, then gave him a thumbs up. We both sat back down ready for the next group.

Before too long the groups of trick-or-treaters faded. I stood up to go in and call it a night. I looked across the street, and Mr. Hawkins was getting up to go in as well. I waved, and he gave a bow for his performance. I clapped for him as he waved back.

The next day. I went outside looking for toilet paper in my trees, and egg goop on my windows. After all that laughing last night, I was afraid there would be revenge.

I heard Mr. Hawkins' front door close and saw a lady walk to her car. Mr. Hawkins must be up, so I decided to go over and let him know how much I enjoyed his scaring last night.

I walked across the street. "Good morning," I said to the lady getting something out of the back seat of her car.

"Good morning."

She pulled out a 'For Sale' sign and placed it in the front yard.

"Is Mr. Hawkins moving?" I asked.

"Oh, you must not have heard. Mr. Hawkins passed away about two weeks ago. I'm selling his place for his son."

ABOUT MICHAEL GRAHAM

Michael Graham is a middle child that has lived in the same town his whole life. He loves to write children's fiction. As an artist, he has one published drawing. He has discovered that the art of drawing is a coarse life. His love of storytelling quickly became a new love, as he put pen to paper. Joining both his drawing and storytelling his art grows.

THE LIFE DEBT

APRIL BROCK

I sighed as I watched Harris pace their living room. He was clearly unhappy with the plan. "He said to come alone, or she dies. I don't have a choice."

"The old Elm Creek Church? Alone? Joseph, have you misplaced your brain? That's the heart of Ambrose's territory. He doesn't care about her, she's simply his means to your end. He aims to kill you." Harris stopped pacing and turned to face me, his oldest friend. "You've always been reckless, but this is verging upon idiocy. It's obviously a trap."

I stood and grabbed Harris by the shoulders. "Of course, it's a trap. He can't take me in a fair fight. He'll have his underlings do his dirty work for him. Regardless, I must go."

"Why does it have to be you? The Hallowed could handle this. Ambrose's pack violated law going after her."

"They didn't bring her into this. The fault is

mine. I knew better than to think I could be a part of her world. If it weren't for me, she'd have been safe."

"It's not your fault. No human should have been anywhere near there at that hour."

"We've gone over this. Her pathetic car broke down. And thanks be to God it had. If she hadn't walked by, I'd be well and truly dead."

"Don't be dramatic, Joseph. You'd have broken free long before the sun rose."

"From silver chains? Be serious, Harris."

"I am serious, very much so. She's just a human. You owe her nothing."

"I owe her my life and I'll be no man's debtor. I'll protect her until…."

"Until you get yourself killed." Harris slammed his fists against the table, getting to his feet. "Dead men can't owe a life debt."

Red heat boiled in my gut. We didn't have time for this, I had to get to Lizzie. Nor did I want to hear him talk about our differences; ones that prevented us from being all that I wished her and me to be. Dragging fingers through my hair, I looked up to the pained eyes of my best friend and smiled, "You dented my table."

Harris had the good graces and enough blood to blush. "It's been 250 years and your idealism still gets us into fights."

"Only 241, and you didn't have to come with me."

"Just like I don't have to come with you now, but I will be no coward. You won't go alone."

I was overwhelmed by his loyalty and it rendered

me speechless. I locked eyes with him and held my hand out. I only hoped it said the things I couldn't find words for.

His hand gripped mine. "This is going to get messy."

"Aye." I nodded. "Let's feed and change, we'll meet back in one hour."

Harris headed for the door, grabbed the handle, and then faced me. "You'd better not get me killed again."

My laughter joined with his.

An hour later Harris and I walked through the wrought-iron gates of the cemetery. Every fiber of my body echoed the anger coursing through me. If anything happened to her I'd never be able to forgive myself. Star-crossed as we were, she meant far more to me than I should have allowed her to.

Howls filled the night air before we'd even caught a glimpse of candle flames in the window.

"I told you he wouldn't come alone." Harris clenched his fist. "The yellow liar."

"I didn't exactly uphold that part of the bargain either."

"Making a deal with the devil only gets you burned." He grabbed my arm and pulled us to a stop. "Are we really going to do this over some human girl?"

I shook my head. He just didn't understand, and I was without an explanation for him or myself. "Yes."

We walked up rickety steps as the doors opened. I ignored the two men holding them. I could see straight to the stage. Lizzy sat tied to a chair, a ratted cloth knotted in her hair covering her eyes. Tears streamed from underneath it, and the stench of her fear caused me heartache.

Ambrose sat casually reclining on a pew. "I half expected you not to show."

Harris grabbed my elbow and held me still. His calmness holding my ferocity in check. "Let her go, Ambrose. Our quarrel doesn't involve her."

"Joe." Her voice was raw and staked me through. "You have to get out of here. It's a—"

In the space of a breath, he'd jumped to her side and hit her so hard the chair fell backward and splintered. She didn't move. Any restraint I'd had evaporated. Diplomacy was no longer an option.

I flew toward him aiming my teeth at the pulse below his ear. A hair-covered brute met me near the second pew. His claws raked at my chest and we tumbled to the floor. The thud mingled with Ambrose's laughter.

Scuffling broke out behind me and I knew Harris was engaged as well. I glanced toward where he'd last been and was rewarded by the sting of a claw splitting my cheek. With a quick jerk, I removed the offending finger's arm from its owner. The man's howl was cut short as I ended his suffering.

Footsteps sounded from every direction. It was an ambush, we were surrounded. The world shrunk to a chaotic swirl of claws, fur, and fangs as we fought for our lives. Tonight, luck was with us, I was still breathing, and from the colorful language behind me, so was Harris.

"That's enough," Ambrose shouted as a man rushed me from the side.

His command to stop was nothing more than background noise amongst the sounds of battle. I caught the werewolf mid-air. I screamed my vengeance to the seething man leaned against the podium and bisected his best lieutenant. I dropped the halves and felt someone touch my back. I whirled around to confront my next attacker but stopped as familiar pale eyes met mine. Harris.

I searched the room and found no one alive but him and me. "Not bad, old friend. Are you all right?"

He smirked. "Only a few bites and scratches, but I may never get the taste of these dogs out of my mouth."

The sound of shattering glass drew our attention to the front of the desecrated sanctuary. Ambrose was gone.

Harris took a ragged breath. "Typical British scum. Start a fight and when losing run away."

He continued his centuries-old tirade, but I ignored him and ran to Lizzie's side. I rested my cheek above her lips. Relief washed over my body as her breath graced my skin.

"Lizzie, wake up. Sweet woman, open your eyes." I untangled the blindfold and threw it as far away from her as the wall would allow me. I pleaded with her to come back to me. "Darling, please."

Her eyes opened, moving frantically.

"It's all right, I'm here. You're safe now." I cooed and stroked her face.

She put her hand on my arm where my shirt had been sliced. "You're bleeding. What happened?"

Before I could answer, her eyes landed on the destroyed room. A scream tore from her lips and her whole body began to shake.

I pulled her face to my chest. "It's all right. Don't look anymore. Your eyes were not meant to bear such evil."

"I...I...oh, Joe."

She wrapped her arms around my neck and I'd never felt such joy.

I pulled her into my lap, held her tight, and rained kisses on her forehead.

"Huh, hum." Harris stood in between the pews rubbing his neck and staring at his toes.

Lizzy's body seized against mine. I tried to keep the sudden rush of embarrassment out of my voice as I calmed her. "It's okay. It's only my friend."

I kissed her cheek and rocked her against my body until I felt her relax. Harris cleared his throat again. I dreaded meeting his eyes, expecting to see fury, disappointment, or revulsion. Instead his arms were now crossed over his chest as amusement pulled at his features.

Smiling in return, I shrugged my shoulders. He shook his head and came to sit next to me.

Without looking, Lizzy pulled one arm off my neck and gripped Harris's bicep. "Thank you for coming with him."

I can't remember the last time he'd let a human touch him. His wide eyes said it had been a long time. When he managed to get his jaw off the floor, he gave her a soft pat on the hand.

"Take her home, Joseph. I'll clean up here."

He dismissed my attempts to argue and tilted his

head toward the door. He clapped a hand on my shoulder and walked me out. I faced him but couldn't bring myself to speak.

He looked from her to me and smiled. "I ruined my favorite shirt."

I leaned my head against her hair and sighed. "I owe you for far more than just the shirt."

ABOUT APRIL BROCK

April Brock is a US Army Veteran who lives in Oklahoma. Together with her husband she raises four rescue dogs. When she's not creating magical worlds on the page, she daylights as a cashier at Walmart.

She is the 2019 Treasurer of the Board for the Joplin Writers' Guild and on the board of the Ozarks Writers League.

HARVESTING SOULS

BILLIE HOLLADAY SKELLEY

In Jasper County, Missouri, the oldest standing building is found,
on the northern edge of Carthage, resting on troubled ground.
The red brick Kendrick House is shrouded in spectral mystery -
enduring as one of the most haunted domiciles in Ozark history.

Around this mansion, fall-flowering mums wave in the wind -
a scent poem of autumn perfume they invitingly send.
But like the magician who uses misdirection to deceive and distract,
Kendrick's crimson blossoms conceal dark truths and bloody acts.

A quick glance at the October exterior reveals

nothing amiss -
solid walls cradle glass windows in beckoning bliss.
But if these old brick walls ever attempted to speak,
the terrible secrets they would undoubtedly leak.

Construction of the home, completed in 1854,
featured oxblood paint staining the oaken floor.
None then could imagine a need for revival -
but donning different faces has been key to
Kendrick's survival.

At times a home, where various families would
abide,
but Disease visited often, and many children died.
Too young these souls left the world and the light of
day -
though at Kendrick, the haunting cries of their
spirits still stay.

Shadowy figures of long-suffering and hanged
slaves,
still can be seen walking, escaped from their graves -
Searching for the sweet air of freedom to inhale,
but tormented forever knowing their mission will
fail.

Once a courthouse, an infirmary, and a hospital
during the Civil War -
Kendrick has witnessed numerous scenes of
barbaric gore.
Civil War doctors amputated limbs on the dining
table top,
placing buckets below for the rivers of blood that

would not stop.

Ghosts of wounded soldiers are seen roaming the grounds -
crying out with an agony that knows no bounds.
Phantoms arise regularly from Kendrick's bloody past,
exposing tragedies and secrets that leave visitors aghast.

Apparitions continue to move lacy curtains to and fro,
hoping to attract the living and convey their stories of woe.
Never showing any partiality for God's light or the Devil's night -
focusing only on the sins of men and their unending plight.

Today, Kendrick is a coffin of bricks two stories high -
a secluded sanctuary where suffering spirits remain nigh.
Blood flows deep through this old house on a hill,
and those who've encountered its specters believe it always will.

ABOUT BILLIE HOLLADAY SKELLEY

Billie Holladay Skelley received her bachelor's and master's degrees from the University of Wisconsin-Madison. Now retired from working as a cardiovascular and thoracic surgery clinical nurse specialist and nursing educator, she enjoys focusing on her writing. Her work crosses several different genres and has appeared in various journals, magazines, and anthologies in print and online—ranging from the *American Journal of Nursing* and *Harvard Magazine* to *Chicken Soup for the Soul* and the *American Aviation Historical Society Journal*. She also has written eight books for children and teens. Connect with Billie at www.bhskelley.com.

www.ingramcontent.com/pod-product-compliance
Lightning Source LLC
Chambersburg PA
CBHW020249150626
46552CB00020B/724